THE UNHEARD

CONFINGO PUBLISHING

THE UNHEARD

My dear Yue

with love

Anne

ANNE WORTHINGTON

First published in the UK in 2023 by Confingo Publishing

249 Burton Road, Didsbury, Manchester M20 2WA

www.confingopublishing.uk

Copyright © Anne Worthington 2023

Anne Worthington has asserted her right to be identified as the author of this Work in accordance with the Copyright, Designs and Patents Act 1988

Cover design by Leah Leaf

Cover image by Anne Worthington

Typesetting by John Oakey

Printed by TJ Books Ltd

A CIP catalogue record for this book is available from the British Library

ISBN 978-1-7399614-8-0

2 4 6 8 10 9 7 5 3 1

For Alex

PART ONE

1999

PART ONE

TOM

If I sit here, nothing can happen. I can't spend money I
don't have. I am safe here. Ghosts came one day and pulled
at my shoes, and when they finished having their fun with
me, they flung me to the ground. She would not believe me.
She said I tripped on my shoes. But I tell her, ghosts have
gathered around this place, and that bodes ill. But she won't
have that either.

The doctor came and I told her about the ghosts. The
doctor looked at my wife more than she looked at me. In
the end, I bared my arms and said, 'See these? There are
things crawling inside and they are itching at me. I get no
rest, not even at night. I should not have to live like this.'
And she blazed her eyes on me and said, 'There is nothing
living under your skin.' And I was going to say more 'cos
anyone can see there's something going on with these arms,
but the doctor turned her back, and I thought better than
to carry on.

Women come and go. I can't say who they are. They're not from her side and they don't come to see me. What do those women want, sitting on our chairs? I ask, but they just look and write things down, so I say they've just come to look. And we need more than people coming here to look. Something got in this house and changed our luck. I say if these women aren't family, there's something going on. But I don't see what it is.

I will try and think about things that don't upset me. I will look out of the window so I cannot get upset. Clouds, plants, and things with names I don't know now. Things I should know but many names have gone. I think I have lived a long time.

MAY

For half an hour when the sun was low, a fantastic smear of light hit the lower edge of the window. It fused with condensation to form a gold blaze where images of the outside met those from the room. Silhouettes of stripped trees merged into her reflection, and she looked at this for a time before turning back to what she was doing. The sun shrank further, and soon the light had died completely from the glass. Whistles and shouts came up from the street; she noticed this as sound washing through. Her attention went elsewhere, dropping into the disappointments and small hopes that had been squashed down until they were nothing more than heartbeat and blood. When it came down to it, what was taking place inside her felt more real than anything else. She turned away from the window and looked into the room, trying to see what a stranger saw. People had started to visit the house and she wondered what the room said about them. There wasn't much to see, just a table with two place settings, a kettle next to the sink. Not much more than they had come with.

She leaned into the sink, using her weight to lift the wet clothes, and wrung them out bit by bit, and she could see from the sky there was still drying time in the day. The last of the rolling water meant the job was nearly done; and these jobs, circles completed hundreds of times, left her in thoughts that arose from the murmuring of the water, and the kneading and rinsing of the clothes. While she was here, she was awake only to noticing thoughts running through and leaving something of themselves behind, and so be changed, like rock is changed by water.

She set the clothes down and stopped for a minute to

catch her breath. When she found her breath again, she went to the kitchen door and listened out for him but heard nothing, so she headed to the back steps, taking them one at a time. She reached for the washing line and the pain caught in her side. She reached again and it stabbed harder, so she knew not to keep going and backed away. A pair of shoes had been tossed out. She wanted to bring them in because he would not remember throwing them there, but the pain put paid to that. They lay in a pile of dead leaves near the place she'd found him lain out on the ground.

Lain out, gone grey. 'A ghost has tripped me,' he'd said. Cold to touch, was he who was the ghost. She wanted to get him up herself but he was too heavy for that. In the end, she asked for help, and neighbours did what she couldn't do. The doctor arrived when he was back on his feet. And by then, he was talking about his ghosts, and the doctor cast her eyes over him, weighing it all up. And that was another black mark against him staying on after she had gone.

If she had to go away, she would run through everything again. He was still hiding from knowing. Taking an old envelope from a pile on the table, she cut away the seal, squared it to make a page and wrote, breakfast and tea. Lunch was delivered now. The clock said half four had gone. The list went back on the table so he'd see it when he had to. It was still light enough for the shadows to wave along the wall. In only a small time, the light had changed.

'I've been waiting in the other room, listening out for you.' He walked in when the clock turned the hour. 'I'm late today,' she said. 'I have more things going on than I can do.' She went to fill the kettle, wiping her hands on her skirt. 'Are we having the meat we bought today?' He asked her this, but there was no meat. Meat was days ago, and no more than once a week. She went to bring some coal in, and disappeared into the dark air, working hard to settle her breath, which was shallow and sharp, when it should be long, like it used to be. He would come out looking for her, she was sure of that. The cold air breathed on her, finding its way through her clothes. She tried to imagine that she was nothing, in the middle of nothing.

She stood in the yard and spoke quietly to herself. 'I don't know what's going to happen to us. I don't know if I can worry about it. I don't know if I can care.' She picked up the shovel and pain shot down her back. She left the coal and went inside.

'The kettle's boiled.' He lifted his pill pot up and down, rattling it to check. She set a plate down in front of him, and thought about what he could make for himself if she wasn't there, and went back to the list, and wrote, egg on toast, tomatoes on toast, cheese on toast.

'Please eat something, love. You're losing your strength.' He said that and leant across in the old way and cupped her hand. He knows I'm his wife, she thought. He lowered his face to the food. 'Is this the meat we bought today?' He asked, but she didn't answer. She couldn't answer every time.

TOM

If I go from the bedroom to the back, there's flowers, circles, then squares. If I go from the front to the kitchen, it's large squares, circles, squares. It's plain in the bathroom. If I see the right squares, I'm in the right place.

I bought a jacket the other day, and she laughed, and said, 'What does an old man like you want with a thing like that?' I was quite taken aback by that. But she is an old woman, and doesn't like what I like. We went back to that place, and the people said they had a hat just for me. They put it on my head, and a stranger said I was the oldest swinger in town. They said I was a handsome devil, and I laughed and bought the hat. The jacket is black. It has tassels like the ones they wear in pleasure palaces. I wear it in the house, it's such a handsome jacket. I told her she should get some clothes to match and she laughed.

I don't know where we are in the day. Should I be asleep? I wonder if that's what I should be doing. She must be asleep. I wonder if she is. I have to pull her out of bed in the morning. She is not well, I think. She took my hand and said I had to write again. I had to write my name over and over. I could not hold the thing properly. I got through the first bit, but it was hard to think about what I was doing. The thing skidded all over the place and I said, 'Come on, love, you'll have to do it for me.' There are things in this room I should know, but the names have all gone.

She might have to go somewhere. I think that's what they said. I said, 'Is she still my wife?' It's dark in the house. If it's dark, I should not be hungry. When it goes dark, we have finished eating, and everything is quiet. If it's dark, I should be in bed.

There is light moving on the wall. When I watch the light, I am a child and there are people in the house. I have been put outside. I am in the wrong place, and I watch them through the window. The people stand together, close, like a bunch of sticks, all looking at the same thing. Then the sticks leave and it's just the room. I watch the light. The light is playing, and I am pulled in, like magic pulls you in. The light moves across the wall and it shows me someone lying in the bed. Then the people come back and I skip out of eyeshot so they can't see I'm in the wrong place. They leave carrying a log. When I go back again, the light is playing on the wall, and no one is lying on the bed. The light had shown me a ghost.

MAY

She turned off the light in the bedroom and couldn't remember if she'd locked the door. She couldn't remember switching off the hob. The person who did these things was sleepwalking, dropping in and out of a dream. Days came and went then it was time to go to bed again. She always seemed to be getting ready for bed. Too much went on that she didn't take in. She had the loosest grasp of what was happening even though the jobs she did in the house gave her an idea of who she was.

When they had talked, they said they wouldn't live apart, with her in one place, and him somewhere else. They said they would stay together. After all, their son lived on the other side of the world, and their daughter lived away. So they would stay together, and the family wouldn't be scattered in four places. They were the heart of their family. That was what they'd said.

The bed pressed down, and there he was, lying next to her on his side of the bed, his shoulder against hers. She watched him fall asleep. It took her mind away from herself. What she noticed surprised her. In the protection of sleep, old expressions she hadn't seen for a long time passed over his face, and these expressions seemed sheltered from the confusion that clouded him. She watched him and believed this was contact with his old self.

He looked colourless in the grey light. That's how they both were now, the colour lived clean out of them. He was patting her leg with a dreaming repetition, and they lay together as two parts of a whole. This is comfort, she thought.

It was comfort believing he remained buried somewhere underneath the confusion, sharing sight of their days. She needed a witness for these days, and the ones that were ahead, and she wanted to believe it could be him.

After the doctor gave her the results, she'd looked for someone to tell. She walked out of the surgery and came back into the world as it went about its business. And the need to tell grew. She came home and he was listening to old music on the radio. He spread out his arms, and they leaned into each other, and she found the closeness she'd been looking for. The closeness made the words slip out and there was a change in his eyes. 'It doesn't sound hopeful,' she said, 'the doctor said as much.' He led her over to the mirror above the mantelpiece and they took in what they saw. She thought they were noting the moment when she came back with the news. He was still clever. It was why she got angry when people wrote him off. He was still there. It was just a question of finding him.

TOM

Lying here where it's warm is the best part of the day. You can't go wrong in bed. I can't hug her like I used to. She says I don't know my own strength. She gets a pat instead. Sometimes, she gets a kiss but she doesn't like my bristles. She says I pong and that's a bit upsetting. I do my best with all that, and best can do no more. We must make the most of what we've got. One day, we won't be here. I'll be the first to go. I'm nearly at the finishing line. I'm not there yet but well on the way. I don't want to be the one who's left. She is better at life than I am, she should get to stay on for a bit and enjoy herself. It would be a grand thing not to wake up again. I can't keep on like this. No one could. They'd shoot a lame horse. What a shame they won't shoot me. I won't go in one of those treasure houses.

They shoed horses near the old cottage house. Our auntie in the middle of the room they kept dark so we could all see her lying in a box. I wanted to scream. I thought it was a holy saint. We sang and said our prayers. I'd never seen a man cry before. Auntie Gem blew smoke over the box. No way to behave, someone said.

God help us if the women are like Gem and those women who visit us. I was watching my programme and one of them burst in and switched it off. I was watching my brother. She said it was no good watching that thing all day. I watch it to keep away from them. I made a rude sign and that got her out. The one with the bottom was talking all over the house about a holiday. A swimming pool. Clattering on. We used to swim in Cocker Street Baths. One of the aunties took us. It was a terrible place. They had us jumping into freezing water. It was strengthening, they said. You had no choice with the aunties. That's who we need now, the aunties in charge to keep those women in check.

Here we are in our little boat. Let's open the window and have a good day. She can't catch her breath, that's what she says now. I'd have some sympathy with that, but no one wants to listen about my arms and legs and they're the very devil. She is everything to me. I give her a little kiss. One day, we won't be here to say these things. But here we are in our little boat, tossed about in another storm.

MAY

The first moments after she woke up, she felt free, and she drifted in that feeling. It was floatingly lovely, lived inside a pouring silence. Then she came back into life and the pain woke again. Then came the long fall. She was falling now, and the peace she'd felt moments ago was just a speck. She wondered if it was the same for him. He was calm in the mornings before the panic of the day set in.

The day promised glittering brightness, slanting flags of sun pointed into the room. Her eyes stopped at the commode and the walking frame leaning together in the corner. She didn't know what to think of them; the grey hospital legs belonged elsewhere, and so did she now. She was trying to keep hold of the life they had together, and the less she was able to do, the more it slipped quietly out of reach. She could think about this evenly now, accepted this was how things were. She didn't fight it any more.

The mornings were the best, before the visitors came, when they were in the kitchen together, each of them in their own dreaming world. She liked being around the morning noises, the radio, toast popping up, the bubbling from the kettle. Each day came in the same way. The post brought a package for her, a brochure and a letter from the hospice. She looked through the brochure and imagined herself there. Then she wondered where he would be.

She watched him eating, his face lowered to the plate, and the radio played an old tune, and he sang along with that voice that cracked, waving the words on with a spoon, just the one line because the rest had gone, and he sang it over and over, laughing and singing.

They always thought he would be the one to go first. And

that she would look after him. He was older than she was, and she had good health. That was what they'd thought.

TOM

A loud noise rushed through the house, jangling my head, and I'd only just finished eating, and I wondered what on earth was going on. She was in the front room and I didn't know what I should do. The noise stopped, so I sat in my place, as still as I could be. Then it started again. I shouted at it to leave us alone. I went to find her. I said, 'Is this you, making all this noise?' She looked at me and pointed outside, but I couldn't tell what she was pointing at. Then the noise stopped. What with her sitting in my chair, and the noise, nothing was right with the morning. The noise was ringing in my head, I could not think. I shouted at it, but it did not stop like it had done before. So I said to her, 'Come on, love, we're leaving,' and I walked into the hall to find our coats. When I got to the front bit, two women were standing on the step smiling. I said, 'Why are you smiling? Was it you making all that noise?' They said something and I didn't catch their words. Quite a good car was parked outside the house. I asked them if it was their car, but they walked in straight past me. I followed them in, because that is what I've been told to do. The noise stopped, and I think it left the house because those women came.

I sat with myself in the back and the women got into her. Then one came in the back and got into me. She sat too close to be a stranger, so I moved away where I could see her better because her face was telling me it knew something, and she was going to say it, and it was going to affect me. I did not want her to say what was in her face. If I could, I would turn this table over and run out of the house. If I was a powerful man, I would tell her to button her lip then she would have to say her words to someone else.

I was wearing my jacket even though we were inside. I was shivering with the cold, and we sat as close as we could to the fire, but the fire was out, and I wanted to tell her about that, but I caught the words back so I did not cause any more trouble. Her mouth was about to say what she had come in to say. 'I am not a well man.' I said this so she would know not to say it, but it only seemed to make her start. Her mouth moved and my ears would not listen. They listened somewhere else, and soon, they were listening to what I was saying inside. It was going well because I did not hear a thing, and soon, the mouth stopped, and I had not been affected.

She smiled, and I had not seen a smile like that for a very long time. It got inside me and I wanted to cry, even though a grown man does not cry. My ears opened. Her mouth moved again and I hadn't pulled my ears shut, so the words caught and they affected me. I was shaking from the cold, and from wanting to cry.

The words stopped and I was lost, and my heart was going like the clappers. Her face was different now, and I knew everything was over. Now my mouth wanted to say things, and my eyes were crying. 'Are you taking her away from me? Have you come here to be my wife?'

I went to find her in the front. No one had taken her away. Now, I don't know if those women came, or if I made the whole thing up.

MAY

Their house was a world inside a world. Years together, years of life were in this house. The hospice nurse was speaking to her from across the sofa, and all the while, she was thinking about pain. The nurse said the pain wasn't under control. Things were changing quickly now, and they could not give her what she needed at home. But the pain felt lighter. Maybe it would stay like this. It might not get worse. The nurse was making notes, writing her way down the page. She remembered the early conversations when they had talked about treatment. Offering her time, thinking she wanted more. She had surprised them when she'd said she wouldn't go. Now, they were offering her a way out, or so it seemed.

Two nurses had turned up on the step in navy uniforms. She took them to be a sign that something was going to happen to them. The nurse was talking about the hospice and she leaned in to pay attention. Her mind was flying about all over the place. 'I'm pleased you've finally agreed to stay with us, we'll let you know as soon as there's a bed available.' She nodded and said nothing. She had already said too much.

The nurse took her hand and they sat like that for a while, the nurse's hand pressing hers. It occurred to her that the nurse might think she was upset but she didn't feel a thing. She wanted to know how long she would be away. If it was a couple of days, he might manage on his own. The nurse said it would be longer, and asked if there was family he could stay with. But he wanted to stay at home. It was their things that were around them, the way they knew the time from where the light came through the window, the familiar noises outside, and the smell of the house: the lived tenor of their lives. This was the shape of their world, their lives flowed into this. The hospice couldn't give her that, it could only give her more. She didn't want more. There seemed no way around it now.

'What will happen while I'm away?'

'To Tom? They'll do some assessments to see if he's safe at home.'

'What kind of assessments?'

'They'll want to know he can make a meal and wash himself, if he's at risk of falling, things like that.'

'And he'll get to stay?'

'If it's safe, yes.'

'And if it's not?'

'They'll look at other options but let's not get ahead of ourselves. You might be surprised by what he can do.' She remembered the nurse who'd made her laugh. She hadn't asked questions, she made them cups of tea. It was a shame she'd only been the one time.

He came in wearing his jacket and stood in front of them. His presence in the room deepened the moment. There were baked bean stains down his shirt and she wondered if that would count against him. She didn't want to be the one who told him. Maybe the nurses would tell him for her. Was it strange to ask them, because something was keeping her from asking. The nurse stood up to go. She smelled of cigarettes and mints. She could feel the touch on her hand. Still there.

She switched on the kitchen light and heard his feet padding out of the front room into the hallway. He came in looking for her. The pain was burning in her side. It was stronger, seeping further into her body. She got him to stand with her and asked him what he would eat if she wasn't here.

'Whatever was on my plate,' he said, 'but you're here, so we're all right.'

She opened the fridge. 'People are going to ask you to do things, and you need to show them what you can do.' And he started to talk about meat, and got caught up in the words. The pain was taking over. Then he was frowning and looking at the clock. She showed him the eggs. 'You could make an egg.'

'Could I? Why are you showing me these things?'

'Because I'm going to hospital.'

'When?'

'Soon, and I want you to be able to fend for yourself while I'm away.' She opened the bread and held out two slices, and showed him where to switch the toaster on.

'I know how to do all that.'

She put the bread in the toaster but he was walking away.

'And you pull this thing down.'

'I know all this.' He shuffled from one foot to another. 'I don't know what you're doing this for, but I think you should stop now.' He turned his back to her. His hands were twisting up the cloth that was hanging over the table. She put the margarine on the table. The knife was jittering in his hand, making gashes in the margarine. He was upset that he'd put marks in the margarine. Then he was worried that he'd ruined the margarine.

'You could always make a sandwich,' she said. He kept his back turned. 'Or you could get something from the café.' She walked round so he could see her, and put her hands over his. 'Someone would show you where the café was, if you didn't know.'

'I could ask the police.'

She would try this again tomorrow. She was speaking from behind a wall of pain.

'It's all right, love,' he said, 'I'll just wait here for you.' He walked off to the front room.

TOM

I am worried about her and I am worried about me. The women who come and sit on our chairs say I worry too much. 'Don't be upset, Tom, there's nothing to be worried about.' They say that all the time. But I'm on my way out and she's not far behind. I'm a wreck, that's what I am. A bloody fool.

I've been put in charge. I haven't been in charge for a while. I'm waiting for someone, I think they've forgotten about us. I'm watching television now. I watched at the window. Everyone outside was just walking about, no one was working. People do whatever they want now. I'm waiting for the lad who comes with the trays. He might be the postman but he might be someone else. I've told him there's no money here. We don't want every song-and-dance man turning up on our steps. 'Don't worry, you've already paid,' he says. Then he says, 'I'll be back for the plates and bowls tomorrow.' He says that because I'm in charge. It's not easy carrying trays. I tell my arms to pull themselves together so they won't let me down. They're devils, they're a hindrance to me. The food's not very good. I don't know what it is. It's a bit like army food. It would be better if they put a bit of Christmas in it. She's lost the knack of eating, somehow. A bottle of Guinness might get her appetite back but I think it's past that now.

My brother's in the room. I sit as close as I can so she won't get in the way. The photograph books are out, she's menacing me with those books. Those women come in and talk over him. I can hear their tripe better than I can hear him. He drives a very good car. You don't see cars like that here. A car is a measure of a man. We had a car once, I don't know what happened to it now. It was quite a good one, but nothing like his. I mustn't have done the right things. If I'd done the right things, I'd have a car like that. I've lived a long time and still don't know where I've been going wrong. I'm a damn fool. Other people will learn but it's a bit late for me. That's a sad thought.

There are faces I remember, but where are they? Sometimes, I ask her and she fires off one of those things she likes to say, and I think, there must be more to this than meets the eye. It's tricky to put my finger on it. Everyone tells me there's nothing wrong and I have nothing to worry about. So it's best not to think. It's just another thing to get upset about.

Eggs eleven. Well, I'll be damned. Bill's here, and I'm thinking about eggs. My egg days are over. Best butter and new-laid eggs. Who said that? Auntie Hetty, I think her name was, but I might have dreamt that up. Cakes that were made with best butter and new-laid eggs. I can still do her voice. She chased him out with a poker and he came out white as a sheet. 'You'll kill that boy, the way you carry on.' Tearing a strip off Da, and no one dared do that. He needed telling, all the things he did. Life can be cruel at times. Whose son were you, Bill? Whose boy? My da did some terrible things. It beats everything to think that man with the car could be Bill. It's how things should have turned out. If he was with us now, he would have a car like that. A car is a measure of a man.

MAY

He didn't know who they were. Sometimes, he didn't know he was a father. His mind reached past that part of their lives. It affected them both.

The people at the clinic encouraged him to revive the past and sift through papers and photographs, and reawaken holidays, people and places, and talk about who was there and what had happened. They were trying to hold the pieces of him together in the best way they knew. When she took the photographs from the drawer, the faces looking back at him were strangers. She picked one out and passed it to him, 'Look, Tom, you're so young here. They put you in a dress.'

'It can't be me.' He took it from her and shook his head then put it back with the others. There was nothing there for him and he looked blankly through the rest. 'Those people look very old,' he said. He lost interest and went back to watching television.

The last time she'd shown him a photograph of their son, he asked who it was. She told him and his eyes narrowed as if she was making something up. He couldn't understand why she would do that to him. His eyes caught with rage when the photograph albums brought up periods of time he had no sense of, so they shared a new kind of time where some people and parts of the past lived around them, while others faded into nothing. And the less they were spoken about, the more it felt as if they had never been. The people he knew from further back remained with him. She thought he saw them in the house. She saw him speaking to people that weren't there, talking to his ghosts. There was no longer any innocence in remembering the past.

A soft light glowed on the arm of the chair. The albums were laid out on the sofa. At the edge of her mind, she wondered if she'd look through these photographs again and pushed the thought away. His programme was about to start, the elation and surprise as he pulled the chair closer to the television. 'He was a good lad, was Bill.' She asked him a question and he gave her a black look because the details dodged him. She was careful how she asked. She knew the questions he could answer, and the answers that came back were the same most of the time. They came out like a rehearsed speech where he was searching about in a small stock of words. His misery started when he ran out of detail.

She took out a photograph of the two of them from over forty years ago.

'Who's that good-looking couple?' he said.

'This is us,' she said.

She told him she had to borrow her wedding dress, and the tram tracks froze and made him late for the church. Four days, they'd said. She couldn't remember if it had come by letter or if one of the nurses told her. She would be leaving in four days' time.

They sat in front of the television with the afternoon voices, people glimmering on the shine of the coffee table. There was the familiar music introducing the high-rise city, the beach people, the palm trees, his face breaking into a smile as he pointed to the dark-haired detective. Her lungs boiled all the time. Someone was constantly blowing down a straw into a drink. That was what they sounded like. They filled up and she coughed up something bloody into a tissue and it surprised her, this new thing. She didn't know her body could do these things.

A fight broke out and a car drove along hairpin bends

on a cliff-top road. He moved closer to the set, lost inside the show. She left him watching the afternoon detective that he thought was his brother.

At that time of day the sun was coming in from the west and made an array of shadow and light across the kitchen wall. She tried to focus on the blobs of light and shadows quivering and running and couldn't hold them down. His feet padded across the hallway into the kitchen bringing his voice with them. He was asking if they had been to town. He thought they might have done, but he couldn't be sure. Then he was talking about haircuts. He said it was time for a haircut now the visitors had come to look at them, and she should get one too. The time had passed to put the cream on his arms, those concerns had dissolved away now. The things that lived in his arms were as good as gone to him. It was the haircut he was thinking about, and going into town. Then he talked about taking the car, and the car was real again, and suddenly, they were younger.

TOM

All her long hair fallen. How I liked her hair long. I look in to see if they've finished. She wanted to look grown up. She looks up and smiles at me, and she looks older, just from having short hair. I see her skipping off the chair, flashing past before I can see her properly. I go and stand on the steps and wave. I call her darling. She's not one of the faces I see here now. I don't know who any of their faces are. They tell me who they are but I don't remember.

I am out here on the steps even though I've been asked to stay inside, and nothing has happened to me yet. I've been told not to come outside but I have learned something from being out here, and I would not have known it if I had stayed inside. I can see my shoes are out here, the ones I wear when I go out. I like those shoes and they've been thrown about, and I'll have to go and put them back in the right place. If I hadn't seen them out here, I'd have nothing to wear, and I wouldn't be leaving this house again.

The best bit about going out is the place where we go and sit down. We get round to it eventually, and when we get there, they say, 'What do you want, Tom?' They say that, because they all know me in there, and I point at the things that look like little cakes. I give them my purse, and they put a cake in a bag, and show me the money going back in my purse, and I like them doing that. Then we go in the back, and we sit down, and I say, 'Tea, please, ladies.' They know what I have, and I have the bag in my pocket and the tea on the table. You have to be careful when you're out. They always say, 'Do be careful, Tom,' because they care about me, and that's the best part of being out.

Something stopped me in my tracks and I don't know

why I'm out here on the steps. You have to be careful, even in your own home. There are so many eyes watching everything you do.

People say I walk past. They say it's rude to walk past. Someone told me I had walked past them, and I couldn't be sure if I'd done that, or not. Half the time, I've never seen these people before. If I've upset anyone, then I'm very sorry about it. It's upsetting to be told you're wrong all the time. And I am always in the wrong, and that's enough to make anyone give up. So I just sit down and keep out of their way now. Then they say I don't speak.

MAY

She only tried to eat when she was on her own. It upset him that she couldn't keep food down. She stood at the sink and swallowed some milk, and it caught at the back of her throat. She shut her eyes and it slid uncomfortably down. The telephone was ringing, and she let it ring, and made herself take small mouthfuls until the glass was drained. She set the glass down, and the milk came splattering into the sink.

Her body had chosen for her. The body was the biggest mystery of all. Every day, she tried to do nothing that would awaken the pain. Pain stretched every hour. She did not know how to live this new kind of time. She thought about the days ahead, and wondered how she would cope. She shouted at the pain, and the pain shouted back. Sometimes, the pain would lie low then it rose again and screamed at her. It scolded and harried her. She had two faces. One face, she turned towards the world, and the other was turned towards the pain. And the pain promised it would fill her until it became everything. It said she was foolish to think this was the worst.

She had lived this long and her body had been silent but her body was raging now. And she had lived this long trying to do the things that had been expected of her, thinking that was what everyone did. And the life she had taken as hers had dropped in her path, and she had picked it up thinking it was meant for her. And the happiness she thought would come held on to its silence, it lived on in her imagination. Her body was giving out now, and she had not properly lived. It was the first time she had taken these thoughts and held them in her hands and looked at them.

TOM

I was told this was an important day but it's been a terrible day. I had to wear a clean shirt. Some people have been in. I could not tell them what they wanted to know. They asked me, which time was the last time? But I couldn't tell them what time it was. They asked me, who is this, and who is that? And I could not say. Everything they asked was in words, and some words are only sounds to me now.

I am keeping out of the way now. They wanted me to make some food. I thought they must be hungry so I tied on my apron. I saw the things we use by the taps, the other things were all hidden by doors. I began with what I could see then it wouldn't go wrong. I saw the cups and forks and they went on the table. There were those things we put on the table that the plates sit on. The things with the cars on them. I put one on her place, and one on mine. I put one cup and two forks on top of two cars. I know we use the cooker so I switched it on and looked for food. There's a box we use in the morning, and I thought, this is what we will eat. Everything was going well. I couldn't see what we used for that kind of food, so I used the cups. Then there was the milk and that lives in a jug.

I lost where I was up to. I didn't know what to do. The woman said it was fine to eat out of cups. She said I should not use the cooker. She said I could have morning food all the time. She wouldn't eat what I had made. I felt a bit upset about that.

Sometimes I see backwards. I see a child in the house and he looks like Bill. Just the way he looked before he left us.

Bill wasn't there for his meal, and no one said a word, and he didn't come back to sleep in his bed. He wasn't there in the morning. I thought about it, but thinking made no sense, so I listened out for their words, but no one said anything. When I asked, they stopped what they were saying, but they wouldn't say.

I sat on the corner wall where our street met the main street and looked out for him. I went there every day, and I watched even when there was no hope in watching. No one can just disappear, not when they're made of skin and blood. I was a kid and nothing was said to me. His bed came out and there was nothing left to say he'd ever lived. It made no sense to me. My home was his home. We were brothers. He was such a large part of me. I was sure he would come back. When I was older, I remembered that log coming out of the house, and I stopped waiting.

MAY

New things were happening all the time. Lunch came every day, and it wasn't from the church crowd, and it didn't come from the neighbours. It arrived all measured out, like a machine had sausaged-out hundreds of meals at a time. A few days in a row, she had worn the same clothes. She couldn't do much, so she watched cartoons and daytime shows on TV, pressing the button to make the television change like flicking the pages of a book. She would be leaving soon. She had to do the rest of the day and two more, then an ambulance would come and collect her.

She could see him in the living room, sitting in the chair with all his things around him. The sound on the TV was turned high. He was watching sport then it cut to the adverts. His hand reached out to the figure on the screen. The figure turned away and walked out of the scene. He was crying and she wondered what he saw. She thought about what she would say to him now they had done the assessments. She looked into the space where he was sitting and couldn't fasten on the right things to say. There was too much fog around him. Sometimes, she couldn't reach him. Sometimes, the way his mind worked disoriented her.

She went to the bedroom and closed the door on the TV sound. She had never been to bed at this time of day. The room emptied of everything except the yellow slit under the door. Then her eyes became shrewd to the dark and she stared at the lines of shadow on the wall. She got into bed with her clothes on and her body sucked down on the mattress. She was awake, and not awake at the same time, picturing her life as a series of images. She couldn't make them continuous. The episodes of her life, stories she leant on as if they were something solid, were evaporating now. It was as puzzling as the fog he was lost in. Everything was turning into fog.

She woke up and felt him next to her. Her body was ringing in pain. Rivers were running down her chest on to the sheet, and her breath came in gasps. She wanted to move but her body had clenched up, and she could not free herself. She tried to breathe into the tight dark spaces, but the pain was forcing itself on her. This must be the beginning of something, she thought, and she tried to breathe, but there was no space for that. Her hair was wet and the sheet felt wet. And her heart and ribs were squeezed tight, and the pain was fast and brimming over, and her fear was brimming over, and nothing felt real. Her hands were fists, and her heart was a fist, and her heart jumped hard and she fell further. The pain was running out of her skin. She tried to think, but words were just sounds, and without words, she felt lost, and her jaw had opened wide, and she might be screaming. Her heart hammered away in the darkness, and she wanted to breathe but could not breathe, and she wanted to open her eyes. Fear had seeped into everything. She heard herself gasping and opened her eyes, and stared out into the darkness.

Her heart lunged hard, and pencils jabbed away at her fingers. Words were turning over somewhere but they were just sounds that had no shape. Her mind was splitting, a crack appeared and she fell further still. Everything on the outside of her was just images and sound. If she could just move her body, she might keep some sense of real. She had not fallen so far yet.

The smell of the night, and the creeping wet of the sheet, and the smell of her body fighting; these were the things she could hold on to at this moment. After a while, her breathing became small and ragged, and everything else sort of rolled away, and she almost felt good. Then she didn't feel anything at all and wanted to sleep, but sleep wouldn't come. There was heat on her face. It must be sunlight, she thought, and she opened her eyes and found the heat was coming from inside her. He was standing there looking at her.

'Help me get up.' She raised her arms, and he pulled her up, and she used the frame to walk to the window, looking for something to put in front of what had just happened. The pencils were leaving and her mind had loosened a bit.

The night sounds folded away and his reflection watched her. Neither of them said anything. The man in the glass watched, he seemed to press on her, wanting something. She didn't want words. She didn't want him to start spilling out words, expecting her to find words back. She looked out on to the street. All the houses were dark. They were the only people awake.

It would be morning soon and the fight would start again, against the pain and the things she could not do, and the fear set free a little. Out of nowhere, she hated him for not being able to help her carry on. And for the way he was, for adding to the pressure instead of taking it away. And the fist around her heart tightened, and she knew she must not think. His feet shuffled away, and she relaxed and waited inside her own space.

He came back into the room and sat on the bed, and the clock murmured, get away, get away. 'Here we are, love, in our Golden Hind, tossed about in another storm.' She waited inside the space, listening further out than the clock. Not even a car went past.

There may have been a few times that she couldn't remember now, but she didn't think she had ever seen this hour of the day.

TOM

Everything I touch is full of holes. I went in the room to find her. I wanted to tell her something, and I said, 'You can call me a fool, because that's what I am. I am a bloody fool.' I said it so everyone will know. It's what I am. A bloody fool.

I said it, and I kept on saying it. I went right up to the walls and the corners. I wanted to say it all round the house, and I couldn't stop. I went up and down, saying it in all the rooms. I said it out loud so the whole house could hear. It's how I feel. I've had enough. I'm a wreck, that's what I am. I'm finished. I'd be better off dead. No one wants you when you're finished, and that's what I am. No use to anyone.

I felt very tired. I had to sit down. I won't go in a treasure house but that's where they'll put me. They put you there when you can't help yourself. It would be easier all round if I was dead. It's very upsetting, but there you go. I'm for the scrapheap, I am a wreck. That's what everyone thinks and it's very hard to take.

I have been sitting here. No one can say I'm in the wrong place and no one can tell me I shouldn't be here. I would like to see someone but no one has come. Even those women would be good. Just to talk to someone. I get my coat and stand on the steps. It's good, I suppose, to be outside. They like to tell me it's not good to stand, but nothing's happened yet. It would be wonderful to see someone. Just a wave would be good. I don't know how long I've been standing, I think it's been a long time. My eyes are watering with the light. A man's walking up our road. I think he's looking at me. I wonder if I know him, the way he looks at me. He smiles, and I say to him, 'Are you all right, lad?' And he says to me, 'Are you all right? I saw you standing at the door. I didn't know if you were all right.' I don't know what to say. It's good of him to come to the door and have a chat. The man is still here, and I say to him, 'That smile of yours is like a good meal to me.' And he laughs, and when he laughs, I laugh. His eyes are bright. Then it's his turn to say something, and he says something, and I miss what he says. He holds his hand out and says he is called David.

'David.' I asked for someone to come and David came. David smiled at me and that's meant a lot to me but I am cold now. I hold my hand out and David takes hold of my hand. 'I think you're very kind,' I tell him. He's someone I'd like to see again but it's time to go back in. I want to tell him something, but I can't say it, so I wave to him. He might know I was going to say something but he's walking away. I asked someone to come and David came. It's turned into a good day.

I know what I wanted to say now. 'Do you have a family?' I say it to him, but he's gone past the gate. I think having a family was something that went right for me and I wanted to tell him that.

MAY

She woke up and found him standing by the bed. She had managed to crawl into another black and white morning. She tried to say something, but he'd been upset when he heard the way her voice had changed. In only a day, her voice had become a scraping sound. She found his hand to hold. There was a loneliness she didn't want to feel, or know how to step out of. The pain was numbing her away. Her legs and arms were lost, greyed out by the pain. To think how many times she'd lain in bed shouting at the pain, and the pain shouting back. Her body rang with the poem of the pain. It made a wall around her, and nothing could get behind the wall. She had forgotten what was on the other side.

She woke later and waited for the sounds to give themselves away and drop her back into the drift of things. She looked over to the space on his side of the bed. She needed him to help her get up but he wasn't there. She needed him more every day. Perhaps that's who they were to each other now. She wanted to show him where she kept the money she'd put away. There was forty pounds. He could use it if he wanted to visit her in a taxi. There would be enough for a couple of visits then they'd be done.

The things that had been keeping her mind busy were not so interesting now. She was more interested in watching the pictures as they passed through. They came up on their own; she didn't have to think about them. They came to her more easily than sleep. And underneath them, the pain was rushing, wild and alive. She felt lighter now, more open. It felt as if the pain was scratching her out. It had scratched holes in her, and she had fallen through the holes, and was floating free now, like a feather blown in. She watched the pain rushing below, and floated higher, the feather. The pain was blowing her further out. And the pictures washed in and they were entertaining. She thought she must be dreaming. But it was impossible to be around so many people in a dream. She'd never heard voices in dreams before, but people were talking to her. And she must have been able to get out of bed after all because she was at work again. All the time that had gone by, and she was back at work.

She found her tongue curled up in the roof of her mouth, bone dry. It felt the same as her throat, but she had no need for them now that the pictures were flying about in her head. She only needed these. And her mind walked through all the rooms she'd walked through yesterday, and there he was in the kitchen, sitting and waiting and talking to his ghosts. She saw him, and had to leave him there.

And how many times had she wished for visitors, and no one had come? Well, here they were at last, sitting here with her, all of them, all the ones she cared about, and it occurred to her now they were all here, that they wouldn't be able to hear a thing she said, with this new voice of hers. It was a shame they were only visiting now, just as her voice had given up. And she couldn't help leaning over to tell her mother all this.

TOM

Time has gone out of sorts. I am at the window. There are a few nice cars outside. A bus is waiting, like I am waiting. I don't know where she is. She must be somewhere. She must have told me and I've gone and forgotten. It's a terrible thing to be like this. There are women in the street but none of them are her. Some of them are quite young like she was once.

I think I'll wait outside. I went outside a lot at one time but I don't do that now. I don't think I could cope with it now. I visited houses. It must have been my job at the time. People shouted down the street, 'The man from the dole's here.' That must have been me. They had me tied in knots telling everyone I'd sat on the baby. Pulling my leg. I liked them all and their houses were like palaces. I must have done what I came to do. I walked back down the street and they were laughing behind me, passing the joke door to door as I walked my way back. I think it was the other day.

I like to do my bit in the house but I stay out of the way now. I'm falling to bits. She is not far behind, and she is everything to me. If she goes wrong, then we all go wrong. We're for the scrapheap. My legs don't work like they used to. She says shouting won't help but I have to shout to get myself going again. She doesn't have these problems like I do. It's a devil to know what to do about it. My legs have gone AWOL. I've gone AWOL. I don't even know if that's a word. I think it is. We said it somewhere but I might be wrong. The place with the flies. It was a nasty place. What a terrible place that was. Those women helped me pull up my trouser leg so they could all have a look. I felt a bit quiet when they did that. I said, 'I'm a married man, you know,' and they laughed. They are always laughing about something, and I can't see there's much to laugh about. They crowded around my leg because they were seeing something interesting. It was a shame I didn't have much to say about it, it was getting attention. They asked me how I did it and I didn't know. I couldn't come up with an answer but they had it all weighed up. They said I must have been outside. I remembered after a while. I was trying to help.

The women say they come here to see us, but I say they're weighing us up. They've put black marks against her, and black marks against me. I said that to them and they said I was seeing things that weren't there. Two fingers up to them. One of them asked if I had a family. I wouldn't ask someone a question like that. I didn't tell her, I was too cross. I must have a family. I don't think I've seen them for a while but I might be wrong. They might come and see us soon. And if they do, they'll see we're in a fine old mess. I hope that doesn't put them off coming. I tried to tell the woman what it's like being me. They like to think they care but they don't care. Everyone has a son or daughter who helps them, but we have to help ourselves. And we have all these black marks against us from people who come to weigh us up. They like to see the worst in me. Then they say I think about things too much. And that's another black mark against me. Two fingers to the lot of them.

When I met her, I knew we would be married. I didn't have much to say to her at first, so I asked her to dance. She didn't say much either, and she wasn't much of a dancer, but I didn't mind that because I knew then she was not one for the men. I told her we would be married and she walked away. I told her that, and she left my side and didn't come back. I thought she had gone for good then I saw her somewhere else. She was not one for the men and I liked that. I knew she was not out for what she could get.

It's cold in the house when she's not here. She must have said she was going somewhere and I can't remember. If she's gone to live somewhere else, I should be there too. If I'm not meant to be here, someone should tell me where I'm meant to be. I'm lost. Somewhere, I have a wife.

I think I've been waiting on the step for a long time. A man comes past. I ask him where we are in the day, and he says something but I'm none the wiser. I tell him I think I'm lost, and he asks where I live. I say I live here, and he says I'm not lost. I don't know what to say to that. I ask him if he's seen my wife, but he hasn't seen her. I ask if he can make the house warm, and he walks in the house, and I remember he's a stranger, but it's a bit late for that. He says we need some coal and he will try and see me when he comes past again. He says goodbye, and he's a good lad for helping me out like that.

I am walking up and down in the hall to keep warm. I have been hungry for a long time. You get ill if you're hungry. Waiting is doing me no good. The house is empty of her noise. I wonder if she said goodbye and I wasn't listening. I don't want anything to happen to her. It's best if it happens to me. I'm no use now. I'd be better off dead. There's some tea in the pot but it's gone cold. I must have been here when it was warm. I mustn't have been waiting long, it doesn't take long for tea to go cold. It feels like a long time, but I don't think it is now.

I like to give her roses on a special day. We grew them so she could have them in the house but I buy them on a special day. One time, I gave her two lots. I was at the bit where you pay and they said I could have two lots and only pay for one. That kind of luck doesn't happen often. I told her two lots was a one-off. I don't know why I remember that. Somewhere, I have a wife but she might not live here now. I might have to live here on my own and I won't be very good at that. I am walking up and down to keep warm. Someone left the front door open. It wasn't me but no one will believe that. I'll get the blame and I won't be blamed for that. I go round and check the rooms. It's what you do because anyone could get in. I go past the curtains in our room. Someone's in our bed. They look like a child to me, but that's no child. I know who it is. I say her name, just a whisper, but she doesn't move. I touch her face. I'm trying not to cry. I put my hand inside my mouth, wailing into my hand. I wish I knew what to do. She was the one who knew what we were doing, and I was the one who went along with it. I don't like seeing her like this. She is everything to me. I tell her that, and the other things that are in my heart. Ghosts have been in this house. I did my best to keep them out, but in the end, I could do nothing about it.

I have been waiting for a long time for someone to come. I stood outside but I've stopped looking now. A dream came between me and this house. I think we were happy once, and something happened to that, and things haven't been the same since. I have a picture of how it was, and I want to keep that picture. In time, I might not even remember that. I walk up and down the hall. Whatever might bring her back will answer all my prayers.

PART TWO

1984

TOM

In the car park after work, I try to forget. I wave to people I know. I used to work with some of them. Some of them have their own offices now. I say hello. I ask them how they are. I ask about their families and answer when they ask about mine. But I cannot forget.

In the car, the rain spits at the window. I drive down the same roads on my way home. I'd like to drive somewhere different, not because I don't want to go home. I love May, and I love our daughter, but I'd just like to have somewhere else to go. In the kitchen, I wash my hands, shake off the water then dry them on a towel. May's home already. The sky's turned black and the rain's arrived. The thoughts come back then.

I switch on the radio and listen to the news. May asks about my day and I ask about hers. All in all, we've not had a bad day. May asks me if I've had any more thoughts about my birthday. I think she wants to do something. She'll probably be thinking about a get-together. There was no post today. The paper's where I left it when I went to work this morning. I ask May if she's seen our daughter, and I ask her if our son's phoned. She hasn't heard from him. I don't worry about our son. He's making a go of things, and he wouldn't be able to do that if he was living here.

There was an empty chair in the office this morning, but the number of forms we have to do is still the same. Something had been overheard and the tongues in the office were wagging. It might be something to do with computers, or computer systems, but nothing's been announced. Nothing's been made public yet.

In the stairwell, one of my bosses said, 'I knew you'd

understand, Tom.' He'd seen me on the stairs and took me off to one side. The empty chair is Roy's. Roy Ashworth's not a well man, but our quota's still the same. People were walking past, laughing in the stairwell, on their way back from the canteen. Laughter, and a thank you. 'Thank you,' my boss said, 'I knew you'd understand.'

In our room, I take off my slacks and tie. May's come upstairs to put something away, and the rain's coming down.

'What are you doing, love, standing in front of the window, with very little on?'

'I think something's going on at work,' I say.

'Are you sure, love?'

'I think so, love, but they've not said anything yet.'

The news is on television while we sit at the table. The Chancellor looks extremely pleased with himself. He stands up and ducks a question. It falls back to the Shadow Chancellor and he looks uncomfortable, but he has no reason to. The Home Secretary fires something back and a point is scored. The Leader of the Opposition stutters. The Leader of the Opposition fails to land a point. The Leader of the Opposition looks nervous and he shouldn't do. The Education Minister is laughing at the opposite bench. He is pointing at them and laughing. And the Home Secretary looks self-satisfied, he joins in and makes a quip. He cannot help himself. The front bench are laughing and waving papers in the air. The opposition benches shuffle in their seats. Then the woman stands up and cuts the opposition down, cutting them down as she likes to do, using the tone of her voice. I pull up the paper and blot them out. What a shower they are. What a shower of ignorant, self-satisfied people.

For eight hours, I listened and I read, and I feel tired of all that listening and reading. Eight hours, I read those forms. There were fourteen of us in the office, and one empty desk, and we still have all those forms to do. They are a weight around my shoulders, but I need the job, and I like the job, and I'm quite good at it. But I can't forget the things I read or the things people tell me on the phone. They come back to me, and I wish they wouldn't. Every day, I'm thinking about things I'd like to forget.

Our daughter's out again. When she comes home, she'll act as if we're the ones who are out of line, when she's the one who stayed out late and had us worried. But I won't come down on her like a ton of bricks. I know what happens when a father does that. I'd like to guide her, but these are hard times, and they're changing times, and I don't have much I can help her with for times like these.

I don't mention the things I think about. It would only worry May, and what's the point of that? In the army, we wouldn't talk about the things that got under our skin. It was a weakness to do that. You kept your thoughts to yourself. You'd never want to relax control. Men who relaxed control went under, they took other men down with them. You can't do that, so you don't say much. At work, they sometimes say, 'Tommy, you worry too much,' and I wonder why they say this when I never say a word. But they mean well in the office. The people in the office aren't a bad lot. I wouldn't want to upset anyone saying what I think, so I keep it to myself.

Footsteps on the path, the front door opens. Our daughter's back. She appears for a moment, says goodnight, and won't come in the room. There's a film on TV that May wants to watch. She asks our daughter to close the door and keep the warmth in. She asks our daughter where she's been and who she was with, and our daughter answers but she makes it hard work.

I think about work. I don't want to, but there you go. The other thoughts are far away, the TV saw to that. But tomorrow, the thoughts will be waiting. May wants to know what I want for my birthday. I say, nothing that money could buy, a bit of peace and quiet would be nice.

MAGGIE

I like to ride in cars, to feel the rhythm of the road, be far from everything I am. Cars are lunatic rooms no one understands, where kids can live at night, crowd in, and ride and fall asleep, go on errands for older kids. I should be sick of cars by now. I am. I'm not.

I waited for a car to stop and when it did, I got in. Three in the back, the driver and me. He and me are friends in cars and nowhere else. We glide through town. They pass bottles about to be older than they are, but they're just kids like me. The empty town is a place that I don't know, is a film set thrown down the road. One day, I'll be miles away, and life will be a different thing. I cannot wait for that.

The road moves out of town and the car just finds its way. We drive through fast and flowing light. The road curves out of sight. The car slows down, then we stop. A man leans in, casts a shadow on the driver. Must make room for him and then his mate. Two of us will have to go. Strangest of all, it isn't me. See the ones they've had to leave behind so this one can take the driving seat. And I have to go in the back, his mate squashing in next to me, and they're in charge.

Lots of talk. The air worn out with talk and smoke. They talk around me, I'm not there. The driver looks me over once or twice. I'm stuck in here. If you don't want something, you're meant to say. But say and say all you like. If someone listens, all the good, but not in here tonight.

Some hand touches through my skirt, goes all the way up. Move away, shift my gaze on to the road. That changes the air a bit. Says to me, not talking to me? Think you're too good to talk? Was doing you a favour, you ugly little cow. The words go in, his little knives. They say this, and they say that, laughing all over the car. One day, I'll think of something and say it back. Not here, not while they want to shoot me down. But one day. When I think of something. When I feel strong. The car stops for two girls walking down the road. Might know them, but I don't. They lean across and talk them in. They tell me I've got to go. Says to me, his parting shot, I think you better learn some manners.

This is how it is for now. Was not like this before. Parts of me, the best parts, are fainter now and buried deep. Those parts have no place here. I'm full of things that I don't know, finding as I go along. Better here than being at home, know that at least. My night has finished now. I've gone, already left.

Cars are a secret and a thrill. I remember running out of road, waiting for the crash and tumbling out, baffled by our luck. The shock stayed as we walked the long roads home. I remember places where there were only trees. Lying in the sun. Had never been before we rode in cars.

I remember a kid living in a car. Weird, he was. Ran away from a children's home looking for his mum. Someone tried to talk him round. His blood all over the car. I remember fights and passing out, kids going through the pockets of other kids. And parties, and just turning up, and always somewhere new.

I remember tyres screaming on the bends, riding past our luck. If you've got no money, it's all right 'cos things are shared. In cars, everyone's escaping something. Never felt that close except in cars.

So they leave me here, as they surely meant to do. The car runs through yellow light, and then it's gone, and here I am. Back home to them, to daughter-me, and every night the same. They come home and lock the locks, cut up the food, wash up and start again. They save stamps and rubber bands and safety pins. The TV will be on, laughing away to itself.

I'm a kid who rides in cars to fill the time and fill the holes. I'm a kid who wants to dive into whatever new thing comes along. I was fourteen. I loved to ride in cars. I'm fifteen now, still hungry.

TOM

'I need your help,' says the voice on the phone.

'I'll see what I can do,' I say. There's silence on the line before the voice speaks again. The voice on the line is trying not to cry. She hasn't been able to face the form. It's for her son. 'There's no rush,' I say. 'We can make a start, but we don't have to finish it in one go. We'll just do what we can.'

Rain is starting to spit at the window. I fill in the name and address, regiment and rank. Then we talk for a while before I ask what happened. I'm gentle about the way I ask these things. Eventually she says, 'He was on patrol. It went off as they drove past, hidden in a lamp post. They wouldn't have known it was there.' I can picture the woman who's talking on the phone. You think you know someone just from the tone of their voice and the things they say. And that's rubbish of course, but part of you believes it. In my mind, I can see what happened. I can see her son and his injuries. I ask her where it happened, and she names the city and the hospital where he was treated, the area he'd been patrolling. I've heard these names many times.

When we've finished, I ask for her address. They can check the form, her son can sign it, and they can send it in with the medical evidence. You have to be patient when you're talking to someone. You can't be itching for them to get to the point. It takes time to establish what's happened, and you have to do it right. You owe that to someone. You can't be thinking you need to finish the call so you can get back to the forms that are waiting on the desk. And you can't be thinking about your lunch. You have to be there for someone. You have to want to listen.

I answer the phone when it rings. The voice on the line says, 'What's happened to my form?'

'I'll have a look,' I say. 'When did you send it?'

'Ages ago. I should've heard by now.'

'Can I take your name?'

'I've told you my name.' He must have told me and I missed it. Outside, there's a man walking across the car park in the rain. He looks back at the building then walks out of the gate. How did he get to leave at this time?

'I'm sorry,' I say, 'could you tell me again?' I go and look for the form. He wants to know how long it's been in the office and I tell him the date stamped on the front. He says I'm lying; it's been here longer. The voice on the phone is calling me all the names under the sun. He says there's something wrong when clowns like me are in work and getting paid, and he's not. The man on the phone cuts off the call. Could I have done more? I wish I could, but I wouldn't know how.

I pick up the phone when it rings, and the next call is a bad call, and when it's over, I sit at my desk, and close my eyes, and put my fingers in my ears. I'm back in that place. Something's got to me and I feel like I'll lose my grip. You are my sunshine, my only sunshine. A little tune helps you keep control. If you can get through a tune, you know you haven't lost your grip. Because if you lose your grip, you're finished, and the people who rely on you are finished too.

I sit at my desk with my fingers in my ears, and I'm back in that place, and I don't want to go back. Something was sailing across the sky. I think I saw it before my pal did. It looked so calm up there, coming closer; tiny, silver drops falling from it. They looked so beautiful in all that heat, like a shower of rain. My pal threw himself down. He shouted at me to do the same, but I was so far gone, I stood exactly where I was. Then came that terrible sound, like an aeroplane coming in to land, then that terrific pain down my back and legs. I found myself lying face down. My pal tried to lift me up but I told him to leave me alone. I just wanted to lie in the sand. I didn't hate the sand any more, it felt like a blanket protecting me, and I thought, if this is dying, it's not all that bad.

Then I was being bumped about and I knew I wasn't dead. The next thing I remember, I was lying in a proper bed. I didn't know where I was. A padre was sitting with me. I think he was trying to comfort me, and I think it must have been then that I finally broke down. He said I'd had an operation and I was lucky to be here. How could anyone think I was lucky? Everyone in that place was damned.

At five o'clock, the phones stop ringing and I sit in my chair. The people in the office put on their coats, say goodbye, and drift away. Hilda Eastwood, Geoff Farmer, Dennis Burns, Ron Birdsall, Marion Nickson, and all the others, say goodbye and drift away. I sit at the desk, close my eyes, and put my fingers in my ears. An amputation above the knee. Fragments of bone were lodged in his thigh. A booby trap in a lamp post. A sniper from a window. The shinbone sticking out. No foot on the end of the leg. Life is a fight. Life is a battle. It's dog eat dog, man against man.

I sit in my chair and I'm in that place again. It belonged to the dead more than the living. It was their boots and burnt-out tanks, their aeroplanes strewn about. I was no match for that place. It was littered with the remains of men who were braver than me. I'm sure it played with my mind, pulling out everything I kept buried inside. It had a way of showing you things that could kill you, or send you mad. It had the means to beat me in any number of ways. I tried everything to keep sane but there was no sanity in that place. I never expected to come out alive.

Your eyes showed you things, impossible things. You'd stare into the haze thinking the enemy might be hiding in it, convincing yourself they might be, because lives depended on you. You might see a train of objects at the edge of what you could see through binoculars. It might be a lorry convoy moving to a new position. You'd piece it all together but it was pitching and dissolving in the heat. You'd be thinking, is this real, or a phantom? The CO was shouting, you were terrorising yourself weighing it up, everything you saw was turning to liquid. Sand blew over the desert floor, you'd look for the lorries and they'd be gone. What a terrible thing when you heard that a convoy had attacked one of your positions. You hadn't done your job. You'd got it wrong. You might have tried your best, but it wasn't enough.

I stopped thinking about these things a long time ago. I thought they were behind me, and they didn't come back at first, but they're back now I have to read these forms and take these calls. I'd like to leave on time, but I don't want this coming home with me.

On the way home, I tell myself I helped someone today, and that's worth all these thoughts I have. On the way home, I try and leave that place behind. When I get home, I switch off the radio in the car. I open the door, walk in the hall, take off my coat, and the desert is in my mind. I give May a kiss, go upstairs, take off my tie, change my slacks, go back downstairs and I'm in the desert again. I check the fire in the kitchen, put more coal on, wash my hands, and the desert is taking up all the space. May wants to talk, and I try and talk to her while all this is going on. I don't want her to know I've lost control. I switch on the television, and push the desert away, and make some room, and keep control. You can't relax control.

In the kitchen, we eat our tea, something left over from yesterday, so not much really, and our daughter puts in an appearance, and our daughter's staying in. That's a rare occasion, but she won't stay in the room with us. In the evening, May and I watch a nature programme about salmon, and they are remarkable creatures, how far they go to spawn. I never knew that about them. The people that they get in to talk on these nature programmes have such calm voices. I watch the programmes for the voice alone. They send me to sleep, and I haven't been thinking about anything much until I thought about it then.

Our daughter is a bright young woman, but she's more of a doer than a thinker. In fact, our son and our daughter are alike in that way. They're not like me. What a girl she is. What a bright young lady she's turning out to be. To see her becoming a young woman is a real pleasure to me. Every day, it's a pleasure and a privilege, but she can be very hard work. The best thing May and I did was to have kids. They completed us, and they've brought us nothing but joy. They're a pain in the backside sometimes, but mainly, they bring us joy. We're lucky that way. I am a lucky man in that way.

Our daughter is fifteen, going on twenty-five, five foot seven, and takes me for everything I've got. I couldn't love her any more than I do, but she's always wanting something. Her mother says no and I say yes, so it evens out in the end. Our daughter asks her mother, then she comes to me, looking at me with her eyes. She's brutal, my little Miss Please Dad. I know it's going to happen, and I think, what does she want now? How much is this going to cost me? It's one damned thing after another, these things I've never heard of. She makes me laugh with the things she wants. Just hearing some of her ideas. When her mother's not looking, I'll take a note out of my wallet and put it in her hand and she knows not to say anything, and she'll give me that smile she always had for me, and I know that whatever's happening – now she's growing up and growing away from us – I know that when she smiles like that, she's still my girl.

I used to take them out in the car when they were young. I used to take them to museums, but they didn't like museums much. I couldn't explain things properly, the things we saw. We sat outside and ate ice cream instead. They go to school all week, you can't be learning things all the time, I don't agree with that. I took them to the motor shows and we all liked them. We'd sit in all the top cars. That was something we liked doing. We all love cars. I know a lot about cars. I'd take them to see the vintage cars, the kinds of cars I saw when I was growing up. We had a car when I was a kid. We had the first car in the road. I think it was a Lagonda car. That's a name I remember hearing, but I've never seen a Lagonda since, so I can't be sure.

The car was the one thing I remember from when we lived in the big house. I don't remember much – parties, going out for tea with our aunties and our mum. But the car was something I do remember. I loved everything about it. I would ask my da if I could help clean it and he'd take me out in it for drives. We'd go and see the houses, the ones he'd built, or whatever he was building at the time. He wanted to check they were being built right. He was very good like that. He was no crook, my da. I sat in the front with him and I thought nothing bad would ever happen if he was there.

He had a knack for making you feel safe and secure, when he was in a good mood. He used to say things that made me believe in myself. I was his bright boy. I had the makings of a scholar. He said he could see my brain ticking all the time. I was always thinking, and he said that was a good thing because one day, I'd be a doctor, and I believed him. I believed that's what I'd be, because I didn't doubt him in those days. In those days, I believed every word he said.

The salmon have finished now and I don't like the next thing that's on. It's a load of tripe. It's one of those damned quiz programmes, and everyone on it has a lah-di-dah voice. May doesn't like it when I take off their voices, but my voices are funny. She says I sound angry but I'm not being angry. She says a lot of things, does May. I draw the curtains and keep the dark out. Long nights and short days. What dark days, depressing days. My da was wrong about thinking and a lot of other things. Thinking can become a habit that can sink you. And when you start down that track, the doubts start, and they become part of you then they drag you down. I draw the curtains and keep the dark out and the warmth in. These kinds of days are always dark, and they're always cold. They get into you. When it's time, I go upstairs to get ready for bed. There's light coming from underneath our daughter's door. 'Goodnight, love,' I say. She doesn't answer and I open the door and switch off the light. She must have fallen asleep with her light on. In the bathroom, I brush my teeth and look in the mirror. I smile at the man who's looking back. It's a relief to get to this point in the day, knowing I don't have to think about tomorrow just yet. May comes up the stairs, and all the lights are off downstairs, and I'm pleased about that. We're all here. We're safe and sound, and our son is making his way in that place down south. I'm pleased about that. That we are here. Safe and sound. And that tomorrow is another day. Another day.

MAGGIE

Walk past winter trees on a sunny day. Why does it have to be like this? Look to the sky. Why, why, why, why, why. Tell me why. Life shouldn't be like this.

At school, red crosses down the page. You're throwing your future away. Every line in every book, the lines laugh back. At home, I rip the pages up. The more I tear, the more I laugh. Words lie bleeding on the floor. That's the best I've ever felt. So much for words. They can do nothing to me now. My victory over words, the only one I've ever had.

At school, girls say, he put it where? Ugh, disgusting. Doing that would make me sick. They wonder what it feels like though. They say, I wouldn't let him do that, would you? How long before you'd…? Would you let…? All the time, they burn to know. Is all they talk about, boyfriends, and the boys they fancy. Holidays, engagement rings, and kids. To be chosen, married off as soon as school is over. Anything else is wrong in this town.

In the school canteen, girls sigh. They talk about love, and what they'll do for love, who they'll love for ever. Walking to the science block, they turn hot and red when boys go past. One of them said she wanted to do it but didn't know the ropes. I said something helpful. They were different after that. No place in the dinner queue. Every seat near them, gone. I sat somewhere else. Backs turned, and every day the same. Just one word for me. Slag, slag, slag, slag, slag. Will it always be like this? Girls are not nice. Are not kind. Are not soft. Girls judge. Are unforgiving. I have learnt that. Girls have rules. They only like girls like them. I am not like them. I dance to a different tune. I have learned that.

At home, he puts on the television. The television noise drifts through the house. As soon as he is home from work, the news goes on. Has to see what's been going on while he's been away. What's shutting down. What jobs are lost. Maps it like a spreading fire. Keeping his eye on the terrible world that lurks inside the television. Hurts me, seeing him like this.

In bed, I dream about what happens next. You'll dream your life away, she says, when she comes into my room. But I do wish for something, for something else. Part of me, still alive, but faint, is buried deep. Is buried to survive. That part has no place here. One day, miles away, my life will be a different thing. I cannot wait for that.

Laugh, and the world laughs with you. Cry, and you cry alone. What have you got to worry about? You're only young, she says, opening the curtains when she comes into my room. This is how it is for now. One day, I'll be miles away from here, and life will be a different thing, but this is how it is for now.

I walk home. The girls from school go home on the bus. Back to bedroom posters, back to Teddy, who'll always love them. They look into Teddy's eyes and they see love. One day, a man will show them that. The sun shines down and I walk tall. Walk away from slag, slag, slag. Past the gates, the rooms that smell of feet. Past the field, the bus stop, and the driveways, and the gardens. Away from all the whispers, the backs that turn away, and the silence when you speak. The way they try and silence you with slag, slag, slag.

Past the gardens, and the gates, and the clouds, and the sun, and the gulls in the air. The school bus goes past. Brace for what gets shouted out. Shouts of slag, slag, slag. Not today. Maybe the next bus. Maybe tomorrow. Keep your guard up. Always do that. Comes when you least expect it. I have learnt that.

Up the road, round the corner, nearly home. The bus didn't catch me. What have you got to worry about? You're only young, she says. Today, I'm round the corner, up the drive, and home.

Bag thrown down. No more taunts. No more slag, slag, slag. Just them and daughter-me. Tea and television and bed. Then back again tomorrow.

TOM

The people I work with are all right. They're a good lot. I've worked with them for a few years now. In some places, the people are at each other's throats, and the bosses are at your throat, and it makes everything hard work. It's not so bad if you can walk out of one job straight into another, but it isn't like that now. So I'm lucky with this lot, and I tell them that in my own way. I say they're not a bad lot, considering they're all Tories, because that is what they are. The ladies in the office pretend to get upset when I say that. I say to them, if someone put a blue rosette on a pig, you'd vote it into Westminster. And Hilda Eastwood rolls her eyes, and Marion might get a bit upset. Hilda might say, 'Tommy, what would we do if you weren't here to set us straight?' I can laugh with Hilda, with Marion it's a bit different. Marion says she was brought up to be proud of this country. Then she'll say my lot just want to bring the country down. She makes a lot of assumptions about who my lot are, but as far as Marion's concerned, there's nothing more that needs to be said about politics, and nothing else is up for question. I look at Marion, and I look at Hilda, and I wish I had their certainty. Then I might not feel like I'm perched on the edge of a cliff, about to fall off.

Today, someone brought in a cake. The cake's been cut and they've been busy putting it on paper plates, a piece for everyone in the office. It must be someone's birthday. Usually, everyone's working by now, but today they're all talking. I am at my desk trying to get through all these forms. There are forms here that I should have finished yesterday but I needed to help someone on the phone, and that was time well spent. The forms never go away. I don't know how the others finish theirs, and have time to talk, and take their lunch, and leave on time.

I see Hilda in the corner of my eye, coming over with a piece of cake. 'We need you to start the singing, Tommy,' she says. I go over and we sing 'Happy Birthday' to Marion. I'm not the best at singing but I like to see Marion smile, she doesn't always smile. Marion's gone pink in the face. She seems a thoughtful person but I wouldn't say I know her well. I know she lives in a bungalow, and I know she hasn't married. I know she's a Tory because she drinks gin and orange at the Conservative Club, and that is a terrible drink.

Here we are, out of sight of the bosses, fourteen of us, with one off sick, and the same number of forms to do, eating cake off paper plates because it's Marion's birthday and she doesn't have family to celebrate with.

After lunch, a rumour goes round the office, while everyone answers the phones and checks the forms. I sit at my desk and check the forms and the whispers go round the office. Then everyone leaves with their umbrellas at the end of the day.

They leave at the end of the day, while I sit at this desk and close my eyes, jam my fingers in my ears, and that place goes round and round. I sit at this desk and all I can see are flies. Flies on bodies that had burst in the heat, held in those terrible poses. Maggots eating some poor devil's face. Flies in your mouth, your food covered in flies, a black patch on your back where they lived off your sweat. Flies on every damned thing, crawling in your cuts to lay their eggs. I hated those damned things, but the bodies were the worst. They stayed with me for days. Every time I saw one, I thought that poor blighter could be me.

I get in the car, trying not to think. I get home, open

the front door, go upstairs, take off my work clothes, trying not to let the flies take over. I switch on the telly, kiss May on the cheek, trying not to get caught up with flies. I smell the cooking in the kitchen, feel how warm it is in the house, smile, and talk to May. I read the paper and try not to think the worst.

The next morning in the office, I'm trying not to think the worst. It's first thing in the morning and the bosses are in the office. No one's answering the phones but the phones are ringing. The bosses are standing in front of us, saying there are going to be some changes. When they leave the office, it's as silent as the grave. Fourteen people, with one off sick, have woken in their beds, had their breakfast, trying not to think the worst. They said goodbye to someone, went to work in the drizzle, through the gates and into this building, trying not to think the worst. Fourteen people walked up the stairs, sat at their desks, looked at the clock, and when it was time, they picked up a form, read and checked the form. Then the bosses came in. This morning, there was something different about the bosses' faces. And there's something not right about the silence in the office. Something isn't right about the way that everyone's working and no one's talking, working hard for the bosses, as if the bosses were in the room.

Look at Hilda Eastwood, working hard to please the bosses. Geoff Farmer, wearing a good suit so he can impress the bosses. Ron Birdsall, doing what he can to please the bosses. And here I am. Thinking of something I can do to keep the bosses happy. Everyone is working hard, trying not to think the worst. Everyone went home last night, watched television, talked to someone in their kitchens, trying not to think about the rumour, hoping they wouldn't be one of the people in the office to lose their job.

Fourteen people, with one off sick, check the forms, answer the phones, and at the right time, they'll put down their pens, stand up from their desks, put on their coats, go home, eat their tea and watch television, hoping they won't be one of the three people who will be made redundant by the bosses.

The clock ticks through the day, ticking off the hours and minutes. It ticks us in and ticks us out. And when it's time, everyone goes on their way, while I sit in my chair. I wonder where we'll be when this is over, which of us will still be here.

I sit at this desk while everyone puts on their coats, and wonder how bad this is going to get. Who will be at each other's throats, now the fun and games have started, now the knives are out. That's how I think it's going to go, it's what I think, and it's what I've seen. It will be man against man. I try and get up. You have to get up and get back on your feet. You have to get up or else you're finished, and the people who rely on you are finished too.

I go home and check the post. The newspaper is on the chair where I left it this morning. May's home from work and I give her a kiss. She wants to know if I've had a chance to think about my birthday and I don't want her to go to any trouble. I don't need presents. Everything I need is right here. I set the table ready for tea, trying not to think the worst. I take the saucers and the cups out of the cupboard, being careful not to break the cups. I put the place mats on the table, the ones we got with petrol tokens, and I don't want to tell May the news. I go to the drawer, the cutlery drawer, and take out the forks, the knives, and the spoons. Because I know it would upset May. I put the forks and the knives out, and put our spoons above the mat. I know May will worry because she'll think I'll be worried. So I can't tell May the knives are out. I put the teapot out with the milk jug and the sugar, and I wonder how this will go, and I wonder what lengths they'll go to to keep their jobs, now the knives are out. May is cooking something and it smells delicious. I ask her what it is. She says it's a simple tea tonight. Just eggs and toast with tomatoes with some cheese on top. It must be the cheese that smells delicious. May's a good cook. I can't tell May the knives are out, I don't want her thinking the worst.

We are a close family. We eat together at the table. We eat toast and eggs and tomatoes with a bit of cheese on the top. It smells delicious, and it tastes delicious and, at the end, there are three empty plates and no leftovers. And it mustn't be time to wash up yet, because our daughter's still at the table. She hasn't sloped away because there's a job to do. That woman comes on the television. The woman walks along a line of factory workers who are standing side by side to wave her goodbye. She's walked up to the camera to speak to us directly, and she says, 'Let those who create wealth get on with what they do best. And those who do not want to work will find out there's no place in this society for people who will not help themselves.' Then she turns and walks away.

I push my plate away. I am full of words but none of them are very nice, and none of them are fit for the table. We'd only just finished eating when that woman came into our kitchen. The way she spoke to us was threatening. I think she's threatened us with something. It's as if she knows something we don't know, that will touch our lives and affect us. It's not the first time she's spoken to us like that, and it makes you feel unsafe. And we'd only just finished eating.

The way that woman came up and spoke to us, was the same way the bosses spoke to us today. It's all about cuts, and cutting things out. These ideas of cutting everything to the bone, and leaving no fat on the bone, they're her notions. I knew this lot would be bad news. I said it when they got in, on that terrible Friday when we were eating our breakfast. I've always thought that woman would have a hand in what happens to me. This is a woman who likes wielding a knife and cutting things out. She believes that things run better when you chop things off and cut things out. She believes that people run best on fear. She's building a country that runs on fear. If there are winners, there have to be losers. It's every man for himself. Our bosses learned the words and learned her ways. And now the knives are out.

I need to get up. I need to stretch. I need to stretch before I explode. I can feel all this anger rising up and filling me. Anger is taking all the space. In my body, a thirty-foot giant is raging. It's tearing at me, all this anger that's been squashed down for years. In my body, a thirty-foot giant needs to get out. I'm scared to death it will rip its way out one day. I live in fear of that.

Our daughter came up with something. I had to laugh even though I knew she was deadly serious. She said, why don't we buy an old, cheap car and do it up ourselves? And I could teach her how to drive, and it wouldn't cost a thing, because we'd have done it all ourselves. She had it all worked out. Do it up ourselves? I had to laugh. I know all too well who'd be doing it up, paying all the bills, and who'd hold her hand out for the keys to drive it away, when all the hard work was done. Daughters. You think sons are bad. I was saying that in the office today. If you think sons are bad, just wait till you have a teenage daughter.

The woman's back. My God, she's busy. Look at the way that woman plays with people's lives, no interest in the suffering she causes, just a head full of ideas about how to make this country run on fear. She needs stopping. She needs psychiatric help. Look at all this chopping and cutting. Watching it makes me feel sick. And she doesn't seem to care. I don't think she cares at all. She doesn't see the harm she's doing. All the rioting and striking, the selfishness and greed. She's creating chasms in this society. She's tearing it apart. The hatred, the poverty, and every man for himself. She needs putting behind bars. Will someone just put this woman behind bars? She's a criminal. She needs putting away.

May says she'll switch the news off if I don't stop ranting about that woman. I didn't know I'd said anything out loud. I sit at the table and wonder what I can do. Is there something I can do, now the knives are out? May gets up to do something. I pull myself out of the chair. You have to get up, and you have to stay up, or you're finished. And the people who need you, they are finished too.

MAGGIE

Sitting on the wall waiting for a car to come. Walked up and down and felt on show.

I'm waiting in the cold. Told myself to wait another minute. A minute more, I had to tell myself again. I've done my best, the best I can with waiting. Killed the time and stayed away from the house that makes us feel like we have lost.

I hurt them again the other day. Me, who never was unkind. The woman was speaking on TV. She had the flag behind her. Taking down enemies with her words. Pouring scalding oil on her words and sending them blazing through the air. The anger and the glory passed through the television. Each arrow hit him. A look of horror on his face. The woman's got into him like a bad spirit gets in. Don't let her in, don't hang on every word. I could cry, seeing him like this. Said something, couldn't keep it to myself. Drowning in things I cannot say to keep a steady ship. There are two versions in my head. The one I see and cannot say, and the one they like to think is there, that doesn't hold up to much. Tie myself in knots to keep things making sense. So you see, Daddy, something's got to give.

Then his face was full of hurt and something else. It tugged me back to put things right. No. No. Was me who saw things wrong. I must have seen something that wasn't there. She shook her head, said to me, after all he does for you. Repaying him like that. If you loved him, you wouldn't have said those things.

Here I am, the waiting done, I'm walking home. Sea on one side, houses on the other. Cross the road and down the street with people drinking, shouting, hanging on to each other, and loud in groups, and twos and threes, and no one on their own. Walk through the noise. See someone there I know. Says, I got paid today, I'll take you for a drink. OK, I say. Here'll do, and wheels me through a door. Think fast which drink I want, and when it comes, it's gone in one. He goes back for more. Sees people at the bar, and brings them back, and I have loosened up to talk. The drink is good for that, makes me do well. I cut the smart ones down to size. They egg me on, and others are buying now. And when I finish one, another one is waiting. And everything in me is free of all the chains. I say. They say. I say back. Win the point and hold the table. It just comes out, these lines of stuff from God knows where. They feed me more and I don't care. I've broken through my shell.

More drinks. I have a heavy tongue, looking round the table to find the lines I've lost. Stare out looking for the words, but all the words have gone. My mouth has stopped, it only wants to drink. I reach out for the thing, the glass in front, but it's not there. Stare into my empty hand, they look and laugh. Can't hold the table now, I'm the game itself. They are saying things but I don't hear. They stand to leave, would leave me here. Don't want to stand, but do the first steps well then heave off to one side, dragged across by heavy weights, and everything is up and down, and I have found the floor and have their eyes again. Don't. Don't you all look at me. I kneel to stand, don't make it all the way. The floor pulls me back down, and what they say pulls me up sharp. Still, I'm the one they talk about. A win of sorts. I crawl behind, all the way to the door, hoping they've forgotten me. Crawl out, and hide behind a bin, lying on the car park floor.

And they have joined in, Mum and Dad. Hear them in my head. One of them tells me not to slump. Stand up and pull my shoulders back. The other one tells me to come straight home. Ruining myself out here, marking myself out. I laugh at them, I do, while they make their last and final pleas. She is full of fury now, and he's gone quiet. And next to me, in my ear, in my head, she says, they laughed at you, they always do. Demands I go straight home before more harm's done. She says, it's killing us, all the worrying we do. You know that, yet you're still out here. All your life ahead of you and you're throwing it all away.

I know the daughter they wish they had, their plans for me, thinking I'm that girl. They hold out their hands to help, I take my hand away. The endless distance of what they want and who I am. Look at me, I'm not the one you think I am. I'm not up to much, I'll only let you down. Because. Because, I can't be anything else but this.

Falling, I am. Falling away. Not quite fallen yet.

TOM

In our bedroom, the coldest room, I found some damp in the wardrobe, at the back of the wardrobe. In our bed, I turn to look at the clock. The newspaper dropped on the mat a while ago. It's past the time I should be up and I can't be late. Not now the knives are out. In our room, the coldest room, I've been thinking about Roy Ashworth and mulling things over. As soon as he heard about the redundancy plans, he came straight back to work. That's what they said when they were talking yesterday. It's all fun and games now in the office. In bed, it's nice and warm, and I've been doing some thinking, when I should be up and running. In bed, where no one wants anything from me, I say to myself, now of all times. In bed, no one's asking anything of me, and I can't seem to make myself get up. Now of all times, when I can't be late, and the bosses are watching, choosing who will stay and who will go. Roy was back as soon as he knew about the redundancy plans. That's what Marion said. Then she said, not again. She wouldn't do his share again. She's more reasonable than she thinks, she'll do his share again. Den said something similar. I said, Roy's not a well man and his wife has problems too. Thinking of Roy is what gets me out of bed. It took thinking about his problems to shake me up. I don't want any more problems to add to the ones I've got.

I draw back the curtains and let the light flood in. You are my sunshine, my only sunshine. A little tune helps you keep control. I stand at the window and think about what's in store for me today. Am I ready? No, I'm not. I put my slippers on, have a wash and shave. I use up some of the aftershave our daughter bought me for Christmas. I come back in our room, go to the drawer to find some socks, and look for a tie. I pull out one tie, then another, then the tie May bought me last Christmas. I haven't worn it yet. People have forgotten that Roy Ashworth's a good man. He's not well, and his wife has problems too. I said that, or something like that. I open the wardrobe, trying to be quiet. There's that musty smell again. I take out a shirt that May ironed, my work trousers and my jacket. I didn't say much. It's none of their business what Roy does or doesn't do. He's a good man. That's all any of us need to know. In front of the mirror, I put on the shirt and trousers then the tie. It's a paisley tie, there's a paisley pattern on it. I look at the tie in the mirror. May said it would go with all my shirts, and she was wrong for once. It wouldn't be my choice, but there it is. The aftershave wouldn't be my choice, but I would never say anything. It's nice to be thought about. I tell them I don't need presents. Everything I need is right here. In the dressing table mirror, I make sure the tie's straight. How much would you give for this lad in the mirror? Ten bob? Is that all? He's doing his best. He doesn't look his age. He doesn't wear glasses except for reading. He's still got good eyes. Always has done. He was twenty-twenty in the army. Twenty-twenty, and a very good shot.

I go downstairs. There's no time for breakfast. I go downstairs and put the newspaper on the chair. There's not even time to have a look at what they've been doing since I last looked at the paper. I go downstairs and May's moving about in our room, but still no sound from our daughter. I go downstairs thinking, what are they going to do, now the fun and games have started?

I get in the car. It's a cold morning, and it takes a while for the car to warm up. I switch on the radio and think, what now? There's a man talking on the radio who sounds like me. That makes a change on this radio station. It sounds like he's being interviewed. That's a turn-up for the books.

The man asking the questions says, 'And what are you earning now?'

And the man who sounds like me says, 'About a third of what I used to earn.'

'And who's to blame for what happened to you?'

'Well, the government knew what was happening and they didn't do a thing. They can't just shut their eyes and say they didn't know.'

'And what about the men you used to work with? How many of them are in work now?'

'I'd say, not even half of them have jobs now.'

'And the ones with jobs, what kinds of jobs are they?'

'Same as me, part-time jobs, low-paid jobs.'

'So it's safe to say you're no fan of this government? You'd like to see bailouts from the taxpayer to save your jobs, would you?'

'I suppose I do blame the government, yes. They came up with the policies.'

I drive through gate number two into the car park and I wonder where we'll all end up. How far this will go. I park the car and check the handbrake, lock the door, look at my watch, I'm not too bad for time. I'm thankful to have this job, even though the forms never seem to go away.

When I walk in the office, Marion says, 'You're cutting it fine this morning.'

I take off my coat, hang it up, and walk over to my desk. Fifteen people are in the office, and no one off sick. Roy's at his desk, so there's less for us to do, but I'll still struggle to get through what I've got. I think I heard this right: the man asking the questions said, 'And those who lost their jobs, how many would you say are in work now?' And the man who sounded like me said it was less than a half. I look out of the window, wondering how bad this is going to get.

There's a notice from the bosses pinned on the board. They want to see us, one by one. I look at everyone working away at their desks, steeling themselves for a word with the bosses. Hilda, Dennis, Marion, Roy, Geoff, and the rest of them, preparing what to say. Hilda, Dennis, Marion, Roy and Geoff, and the rest of them, will be trying to please the bosses. Hilda, Dennis, Marion, Roy and Geoff, and the rest of them, will be doing what they can to keep their jobs. Everyone answers the phone and checks the forms, but you can cut the atmosphere in here with a knife.

After lunch, Geoff has a talk with the bosses. Hilda goes in next. She looks relaxed after she's had a word with the bosses. Den is after Hilda. You can see the relief on his face when he comes back in the office. And I'm next to go through the wringer.

It must have been a couple of weeks ago that I told May, and she said I had nothing to worry about. She couldn't see why I'd be in the firing line when I work so hard. It must have been a couple of weeks ago that May said I should relax because my job's not on the line, I don't have time off sick. I was thinking about what I wanted to say, you want to feel prepared going into something like this. You want to be ready in case they've got their eye on you. You can't be complacent and think the axe will fall on someone else.

I walk down the corridor and stop at the door. Someone puts their hand on my arm and says they haven't seen me in a while. A voice from inside the room says to come in. 'Thank you,' I say, and remember to smile. I take a seat and face the bosses. I can hear May saying I mustn't worry. In the seats opposite me, the bosses say the job is simpler than I make it. Sitting opposite me, two of the bosses say they don't need all the detail I've been giving them. I spent some time preparing what I was going to say. I spent some time thinking about what I wanted to say. Now, I can't remember any of it. I look down at the floor, see the tie, and hope they haven't noticed it.

Tick-a-box, tick-a-box. My job is simpler than I make it. My job is to look up values in the tables and write them in the boxes. Check the form, then move on to the next one. Tick-a-box, move on. Tick-a-box, move on to the next form. It's not as complicated as I make it. I'll get through my quota if I stick to that. It's all they want. And I don't need to spend so long on the phone. Questions only take a couple of minutes to answer, it's not our job to do more than that.

Tick-a-box, tick-a-box. I go back to my desk, take out a form, open the book of tables, flick through, find the right page, and look up the value for the loss of a right arm. I write the value in the box. I take another book of tables and look up the figure for the length of service, read off the value, work out the multiple for the length of time ahead and the length of time served. I go to the next part of the form, flick through the pages in the book of tables, read off the value, write it in the box, do the calculation, and check the rest of the form. Then I move on to the next one.

When the hours are up, everyone puts on their coats. After eight uneasy hours, fourteen people stand up, say goodbye, and drift back home, and I don't move.

'You're staying late again,' says a voice behind me, says the voice of Dennis Burns.

'Just finishing up, Den. I've still got a pile of forms. There's more here than I can do.'

'You don't want to be seen staying longer. These aren't your hours, Tom. How do you think it makes the rest of us look?'

'Don't worry, Den, I'm going soon.'

'No one likes seeing you staying back. It doesn't look good. They'll have us all doing it, Tom.'

'I'll see you in the morning, Den.'

And Den is putting on his coat, and Den is walking past, and Den is leaving the office for the night, and the door has closed behind Dennis Burns, and I sit in my chair looking at the floor.

I close my eyes and put my fingers in my ears. What would Den do if he had all this going round and round his head? It's every man for himself now the knives are out.

I sit at my desk and Den's words have given me an idea. They don't want me to get involved with people, but I am involved with people. They just want me to do my quota. They want me to do the job a certain way, and the only way I can do the job, is to do it my way. I signed something when I took this job that stops us from doing this, but I haven't got a choice. I'll take these forms home with me, finish them off tonight, and get to keep my job. I need this job, I'm not bad at this job, and I'm going to stick to this job like grim death.

I drive home feeling tired, and the forms are weighing on my mind. I unlock our front door, say I'm home, put my bag next to our shoes, turn on the television, and the forms are taking all the space. I kiss May, go upstairs to change, and the woman's voice is all over the house. I go downstairs to see what she's been doing. I don't particularly want to know, but I don't want to miss something that might be important. The woman strides down a red carpet while the cameras flash. She didn't used to walk like that when she first started. Back then, she walked like one of those game birds, but nowadays, she glides. Every day I see her doing something. I think I know her quite well now. You've got to hand it to her, she's always working. So many cameras are flashing as she walks down the carpet, as she walks down the runway, straight off a plane. She's like a film star, making a film star's entrance, and she wasn't like that when she first started. She walks up to the reporters, and the first to ask a question is one of the few who stands up to her. But look at this. This is the kind of thing she does. She's straightening his tie, and leaning into him, talking away in that slow, low voice she has. She says it's a pity he won't wear a blue tie for her. And he's stunned. He's speechless. He can't move. He hasn't even asked the question, and look, she's hypnotised him. Like a snake, she is, dancing in front of him. I can't watch this any more. There's no hope for us.

It's six o'clock, and she's already done a full day's work, she's flown somewhere, and she's still out working. It's one reason why that woman's so dangerous; she doesn't stop. She only needs a couple of hours' sleep, and when you think about that, it means she gets all those extra hours the rest of us don't get. It puts her at an unfair advantage. Another reason why she's so dangerous. No one can keep up with her.

May's calling from another room, wanting to know where I am. I'm in here, watching and thinking, trying to work out what that woman's up to, so I can keep us safe. May comes in and says I look worn out. I say, there's some work I need to finish. I know what May will think, but I don't think the same way she does. I have to do things in my own way. I know that woman's up to something. I have to watch so I know what's going on. It's what I do to keep us safe. May thinks I'm just watching telly but I'm trying to keep us safe.

In the kitchen, May and I wash and dry the pots and put them all away. Our daughter's nowhere to be seen. She's probably gone somewhere to study. She has to go to other people's houses to get the books she needs. I'd like a shelf of books, but I wouldn't know where to start. Our daughter clears off when that woman comes on the telly. Our daughter's grown up with that woman in the wings, watching and waiting, looking at us while we're eating at the table, like a family should.

I clear a space on the table and take the top form out of the bag. I don't know how that woman manages to work all day and well into the night, day in, day out. I'd end up in hospital if I did that.

I read the forms and one of them is bad. It affects me quite a lot. I go to the front window and look down the road, hoping I'll see our daughter coming home. I stand at the window and look down the road, hoping she's all right. I go back to the kitchen, sit back down at the table, and brace myself for what I'll read next. I sit down at the table and that place is almost back. I sit down and feel the weight around my neck. It's been a long day, and not a very good day, and it's not over yet. I'm lost in all these forms, getting nowhere, but still employed. I'm thankful for that. I think about that woman. Every day, she must feel the weight around her neck, lost in all those papers. I take my hat off to her even though I don't like her. But you have to be in awe of how she does it every day. I look at the clock in the kitchen and think about our daughter, wondering where she is. I used to worry about our son, but when you have a daughter, it's one thing after another.

I go back to the window, draw back the curtains, and look down the street. The street light comes in the room, and so does the fear. When the fear's got into you, the doubts get in as well, and they become part of you, and drag you down, and choke you. I'm at the window with the curtains drawn back. I wish I knew how to fight these fears and doubts. I'm thinking things over, making things worse. The answer must be somewhere, if only I could find it. I go upstairs and the fear comes with me, and I'm thinking things over, making things worse, but it's all I have to fight these fears and doubts.

It's past the time our daughter should be in. It's past the latest time she should be in, and she has school tomorrow and needs her strength for that. I tell her this all the time, like a record that's got stuck, because she needs her strength for school. I go back to the forms and do the rest the easy way, the way they should be done. I switch off the gas fire. The kitchen fire will go out on its own. I turn off the lights apart from the kitchen one, and think about our daughter. She looks older than she is. The door clicks open and there she is, with her steady, unsteady steps, tottering in her heels, and I'm more relieved than I've felt in a very long time. I hear her in the hallway, then she comes in the kitchen, and I'm happier than I've felt in a very long time. She comes and sits next to me, leans on me, and starts to speak. Then she stops talking, but we don't need to talk. There are things I'd like to say, but it's too late to say them now. She wouldn't listen anyway. I'm just her old dad, who feels happy because she's walked in through the door. I couldn't love her any more than I already do. She looks a bit upset, so I

let her lean on me. I ask if she's all right. She says she is, after a while. It's late now and she should get some sleep. She
needs her sleep because she needs her strength for school.

MAGGIE

These houses where you go and study, what are they like? Have they more than us? I tell him about patios and extensions, and so-and-so's dad in sales, and all their money that goes on nothing. Really? Yes, Dad. They could have lots, but they don't. They're just like us. And your studies? Does it help, studying at these houses? They have books there, Dad. Oh. That's something I can't help you with, love, and that's a shame. You're better off studying there. Yes, I'm going now. Off to study. A little lie. Don't be too late. You need your sleep. You need your strength for school. And I am out before the questions start. Before Mum gets involved. She doesn't believe in much from me.

I walk and walk. Then it's, hello. Who's this one who's come up to me? You don't remember? He stops so I can recognise. Moments go by then I see a house, downing drinks left on the table. Fell and split my head open. It bled and bled. Someone walked me back and things just happened. Never entered my head that we would. Was only walking back. The next day thought, who was that? Did I want to? I must have done. I never said I didn't. Is that this one?

Says, I hoped I'd see you again. On your own, are you? Come with. Go on, I've got a car. Where will we go? Where you want. Come on. We walk. Is this one yours? I haven't been in cars for months and here I am, next to him, this man, drinking from his can of beer. We do not have a place in mind.

The sun is bursting through. There is sun on the pavement, in the trees. The sun has found its way on to my legs, his hands, his hair. I open the window, let the air blow in. This man. This man. Don't know what I'm here for. He drives, says nothing at all, looks straight into the road. Waiting for me to say. I sit and look instead. Out of the corner, see him smile. A smile for him, not meant for me. When he looks over, I let him look. Says, you don't say much, do you? No, I don't. Would not take much to know my story, and easy then for him to find the way back to miserable-them and daughter-me. Him too. Could have a girlfriend, baby, wife. We each have our reasons not to say.

The road turns into buildings and there he stops the car. Promises he won't be long. Says, you can have anything you want when I get back. Takes paper money from his pocket and shows it in the air. We'll have a great time, you and me. Smiles at me in a friendly way. Some kind of friend he is now. Before I speak, he's disappeared. I see him nowhere. Don't know where we – he – is. Sink down in the heat of the car and wait. Is all I can do. My silence started something. I saw it happening and didn't say a word.

I wait till getting dark and more. To the point of giving up. He comes out of some house door. Might be hoping I'd be gone by now. What a joke on me that would be. Have no idea why he asked me here. Sorry, he says. I've been so long, and looks at me, takes my face into his hands. I wonder who I am to him. We'll have a great time, I prom- ise. Brings a bottle out. Don't want to drink. I have school tomorrow and need my strength for that. Just a kid riding in a car. He unscrews, he drinks, then hands to me. I am not. A kid. I prove. I drink. Burns all the way going down. I drink the drink. His spirits. His great time. He lights one up and hands to me. Makes it easy so I don't have to not know the ropes. Something is happening. We drink. He drives. Have a taste for this now I am numb. Remember this from other times. He sees the bottle empty. Winds the window, throws it out. Laughs and pulls another one. I take it from him, hear me laughing, and wonder why I thought he was ever out of reach.

He stops the car. Says, we can have such a good time, you and me. Say, I should go, with hand on door. But you said you were enjoying yourself. Go on. Stay a little longer. His hands do not gently go up my sweater, inside my bra, up my skirt, inside me. Unbuttoning everything, he does everything, I do nothing. I am spinning. Try to make just one of him stay still. Trying not to be sick with all this moving going on. Part of me leaps in, kicks in, saying things it thinks I need to hear, and part of me laughs it away. Forget what is meant, not meant to be. I'll let him if he wants. Pulling me, his teeth on mine, pushing himself in. Know this like a memory I've had. The table, drinking down the drinks. My face on the ground. Curtains on the rest of what I remember there. The curtains fall again. He holds to me, sticking to me, needs me a few minutes more. And all the while he sees me. Makes that known. Feel not alone in this with him. And that's the best, the best of all. Is why I'm here. So keep it. Keep this moment.

I do not know how to fill the silence when it falls. Saw something in my face, he turned away. I should, I want to go now and be back, and be the girl I was before. Say, I have to, want to go now. On the verge of touching him, but he and I have pulled away. A turn, a street, with houses soon. The road slows down. I know these roads. Here. Stop here. It's fine. I'll walk a mile and sober up, keep the best bits of these moments. The car, the drink, this feeling that will have gone by morning. When I peel the clothes off my legs and arms, and see the bruises from the man, something strong will hate in me and something else will laugh.

I wobble in. No thought of going upstairs while he is in the kitchen with his head wrapped up in numbers, while we pretend he's sleeping. I sit with him the way I used to sit when we were like we were before. The smell of me fills up the place. I have to break the silence now. My too loud voice staggering over itself, too full of things and hugging on to him in a matey way, once it has all but petered out.

Are you all right, he says. No, I want to say. I am not all right. I look a long time in the window, his reflection at the table. Not looking from his numbers. I'm all right, I finally say to the glass, then peel myself away. That's good. You go up now, love. You need your strength for school. So, who am I, and who are you now, Daddy? Now we are both so far out to sea? Will you come back to me one day? Promise? Promise?

TOM

I am here, sitting at my desk with all these forms. I'm lost in forms, getting nowhere, but still employed. I'm thankful for that.

I sit at my desk by the window and it's a beautiful day. Hilda Eastwood sits at the desk next to me. Roy Ashworth sits behind, but Roy's not at his desk. Hilda is liked by all the bosses. She's a good and cheerful person. She finishes her work on time and manages to chat. She's going round the office with a card and pen.

'What's the occasion, Hilda?'

'Haven't you heard? Roy's taken a heart attack, Tommy.'

'I didn't know, Hilda. I'm really sorry to hear that.'

'It's serious this time, Tommy. I don't think he'll come back to work now.' Hilda talks. And while she talks, I'm thinking about something and I don't like what I'm thinking. While she talks, I think about pressure. I bet it was pressure that got to Roy. There's pressure on me, there's pressure on Geoff, there's pressure on Den, and pressure on Roy. And Roy is not a well man. It's pressure all the time. Hilda, on the other hand, seems to breeze through everything. I don't know how she does it. But if you feel pressure like I do, there's nothing worse than knowing you're one of the ones they've got their eye on. And if you feel pressure like I do, there's nothing worse than knowing you're one of the people they think could do better. It's a terrible feeling, and redundancy is a terrible word. You don't know what they've got in mind. You don't know how long you've got, or when they're going to come and say, come in number three, your time's up. You want to be ready, just in case. You want to feel prepared. You don't want to be complacent and think the axe will fall on someone else. That's the last thing you want to be thinking. And you don't know when they'll tell you. They could tell you today, but it might not be today, so you have to be ready every day, because the shock will be the worst thing of all. It's the shock that kills you. Look at Roy. He's not dead, but he's not very well. You don't want to get a shock like that, and you don't want any nasty surprises. So you take the pressure, and thinking about it keeps you prepared.

Tick-a-box, tick-a-box. I'm at my desk with all these forms. Getting nowhere, but still employed and I'm thankful for that. I've just got to get through all these forms to keep my job.

Before I left for work, I told May I didn't want any fuss. I said I have everything I need right here, and I hope she understands. In the office, there hasn't been any fuss, and I'm glad about that. The people in the office are talking tripe. I'm hearing tripe all around me. They like to talk a lot of tripe in this office.

'It trickles down like a champagne fountain. The money runs all the way down from the top to the bottom. From the rich to the poor. The rich fill up the top layer, and when that's full to the brim, the champagne runs over the top, and that's the money pouring down to the middle row. Then the middle row gets filled to the brim, and the money flows down to the bottom. That's how it works. Money or champagne, it's all the same. It all pours down.'

I sit at my desk and keep my mouth shut. Oh deary deary me. I sit at my desk and I wonder when this has ever happened. In the whole of history, when has this happened? When have the rich allowed their money to spill over for the rest of us? And when has money ever flowed down to the poor? Oh deary deary me. I sit at my desk and scratch my head. I can't think of any time in history when this has happened. The rich just get their hands on bigger glasses.

'It was how they explained it. Yes, it was a serious programme. This is what they think now. It's how it works, and it's how it's going to work from now on. When you think about it, it makes sense. It makes a lot of sense to me.'

Oh deary deary me. I sit at my desk and think about how money trickles down. I think about what I might say if it wasn't such a beautiful day, and if the knives weren't out. I think about what I might say if there weren't these fun and games going on in the office. If you want to know how money trickles down, you give people like us tiny glasses.

It's Friday. There's a buzz in the office, and only last week, you could cut the atmosphere with a knife. Today in the office, everybody's talking, even though they're talking tripe. Last week, we had to see the bosses in their office, and you could cut the atmosphere with a knife. Everyone has their own ideas about who'll be made redundant, and the way it looks to me, everyone thinks it won't be them. It's a terrible thing, redundancy, and three of us will be made redundant, but everyone thinks it won't be them. Last week, I took my turn and saw the bosses, and it left a bad taste in my mouth. Last week, I wasn't the man I like to think I am. I sat in the chair and I was a humbled man. Last week, the way I sat in that chair, listening to what they said, I felt like I'd already lost. And I can't forgive myself for that. The way I was last week, I was a humbled man wearing that paisley tie, and my head was down, like I'd already lost. You are my sunshine, my only sunshine. I hum a little tune but it doesn't take the nasty taste away. I can't forgive myself for that.

Sometimes, life shows you a thing or two, things you'd rather not know. And last week, I was shown what kind of man I am. The kind who keeps his mouth shut while people say what they like about me. And shame on me for that. If there are winners, there have to be losers. It's every man for himself. That's what it's about. That's life. It's whose face fits. That's what it's all about.

Every man for himself. Those old habits, those old lessons. Lessons we learned from Da. If there are winners, there have to be losers. There are those who get caught, and those who get away. That was the way when we were kids. And where were you, Tommy Pullan, when those lessons were being learned? Hiding behind your brother. And shame on you for that. You didn't want to see, and you didn't want to know. It was a long time ago but these things stay with you, they stain you somehow, even though you don't want them to. Your brother Bill was twice the lad you were. Shame on you, Tommy Pullan.

There are those who get caught, and those who get away. There are those who have lots, and those who have nothing. There are winners, so there have to be losers. Our lessons from Da. And where was Bill when you were looking the other way? Sent out to the yard. You could see him from the kitchen window, sleeping in that box Da built from bits of wood he found on his walks. And when he had a mind to, Da stuck a bit of food and a couple of blankets in. When it suited him. And no one said a word, and no one dared. We didn't want to see these things, we didn't want to know. Because nothing would change Da's mind once it was set. And because Bill had crossed a line. That's what they said. But Bill had crossed no line. And you kept your head down because you were scared of Da. You couldn't look him in the eye. And you couldn't look Bill in the eye. And shame on you for that. The lessons worked. They bloody worked.

And where was Da? In the middle of the room, in front of us, turning to our sister, turning to me, then turning to Bill, rubbing his hands while he was deciding, deciding it was Bill. The relief that he hadn't stopped at me. Two young lads were in that house. One was a scapegoat. The other one, a coward.

Here we go again. It's funny the way these things come up, and you think it's all behind you. I don't want to think about these things but they come up anyway. And that funny taste in my mouth never goes away. The old habits. The old lessons. If there are winners, there must be losers. There are those who get caught, and those who get away. There are those who have lots, and those who have nothing. It's man against man. Every man for himself.

I'd just like to think about something nice for a change. It's Friday after all, it's a beautiful spring day. I look out of the window and watch the light. I look out of the window and steal a moment from the bosses. What a day. It's a beautiful world out there. Never mind what's going on in here. Our son phoned last night and he always makes me laugh. He was telling me his girlfriend has a new job. She works with old people now. She had to stick her finger up an old man's bottom, and he's getting a promotion at work. Good for them. He thinks she'll stick at this job. She's good with people. He sounded happy. He said they're looking for a flat together. I said, 'And who is she, this wonder woman, who's making you so happy?' As long as he has a job, I'm happy. If he's happy, I'm happy. He deserves to be happy. He did what he had to do and moved all the way down there, and our loss is their gain.

'You'd like it here,' he said. 'You and Mum can come and stay when we get the flat. Come down and have a holiday.'

'We'd like that. I'd love to get away.'

'You'll see the sun down here.'

'I know that, son. We always look when they do the forecast. They say the sun shines on the righteous.'

He was talking and I was smiling. Things are different down there. It's like being in a different country. I couldn't love him any more than I do, and I told him that. It's important they know you love them. Then I passed him on to his mother. It's not enough, these phone calls, but they keep us connected, and keep us as a family. He has a job and his health, and I couldn't be more happy for him.

I've had a break and I'd like to get on with my work, but I've had enough today. They say you can't flog a dead horse. Everyone's talking in the office. There's a buzz in here this afternoon. That's a change from last week. Fourteen, with Roy off sick, not caring what the bosses think. And that makes a change. The clock ticks away the hours and the minutes, and I can't get back into my work. Then it's time to go, and everyone stands up, leaves their desks, makes their way out, they'll go home and talk to someone in their kitchens, watch TV, then come back on Monday, and the pressure will be back again.

On the way home, I think about Roy. I hope he'll be OK. On the way, I think about home, and I'm grateful for what we've got. We've got our health, our jobs, we are a family, and I couldn't wish for any more than that. On the way home, I think about what we have. I think about it all, and I wouldn't swap with anyone.

On the way home, I think about luck. It's going to come down to luck. I used to think it was about hard work. But it's not, it's about whose face fits. On the way home, I think about luck. It's all about luck, and Roy is not a lucky man.

He's fighting an uphill battle now.

It's Friday night and I open the door and check the post. There are a couple of things for me. It's Friday night and I'd like a drink. May says there's quite a good film on later, and she says I look happier than I have for a while. And she looks happy, seeing me happy. And I do feel happy. The pressure's gone and I feel good. I feel like my old self again. It's Friday night and we're having a special tea. After tea, I say to May, let's have a drink. I go to the cupboard, take out two glasses, and the bottle, and pour us both a whisky. May says, 'Happy birthday, love,' and gives me a kiss and a card. She asks if I had a good day and I smile, but what happened today isn't a smiling matter. I was smiling because I felt a bit of breathing space. It felt like the old days again, when the pressure was off. I was smiling because I felt a surge of hope, and what a feeling that is when you haven't felt hope for a while. But what I was smiling about was someone's adversity, and the smile's been wiped off my face now, because it was false hope felt by a desperate man. To think I used to believe this was going to be about hard work. Now, I'm reduced to thinking it's down to luck, and I'm putting my faith in luck. I've been smiling, but the smile's faded, because Roy's a good man, but he's had a run of bad luck. It didn't take me long to think that if Roy's off sick for good, that's one post they can get rid of, that isn't mine. To think it's come to this, where I'm grateful for someone's adversity. It shouldn't be like this.

I'm drinking a glass of whisky and there's quite a good film on. It's my birthday today and there wasn't any fuss. That's just the way I like it, but I don't think May understands. That woman will still be working. No doubt she'll work into the night, with her papers spread out all over the carpet, just the way I saw it in a photograph. And that woman drinking a tumbler of whisky, working through the night.

I'm in the kitchen but I'd rather be with May. I'm drawing that face again. I've drawn it many times. I called him Don because he looked like a Don to me. I could see he was Italian from his uniform. He was after my life and I was after his. I felt his fear as much as I felt my own. I fired into his chest and he slumped down. I went over and my legs gave way. I was kneeling in front of him, and I could see he would be dead quite soon. I had no idea why it was him lying there and not me. He looked as if he was smiling. How I would have liked him to raise a hand, I would have shaken it. After all, we'd seen the same things.

He was my enemy and I thought I should hate him, but I could hate nothing about him. In fact, I wanted us to be friends. There were so many things I wanted to know about him, seeing as our paths had crossed like this. I thought he wouldn't mind me looking in his jacket, so I put my hand in his inside pocket. There were letters and a photograph or two, and I took them out. He would have done the same to me. He was better looking than me in every way, I bet he'd charmed some women. I spied a bottle of their wine underneath some magazines. 'You'd want me to have a drink, wouldn't you?' I nodded in his direction. One army fed off another. We were all the same. It was man against man. I called him Don. He was my first one, and on my nineteenth birthday too. So we're linked, me and him. And of all the days, it had to happen on this day. So it's never just a birthday for me, I don't want a fuss. I wish it had never come to that, but there it is. He was such a handsome lad. I raise my glass to him and open the post, put the cards on the mantelpiece, put the drawing on the coals, and watch it turn to fire.

MAGGIE

Not every part of me is travelling the same speed. The wanting part is far ahead. I'm wanting all the time. I want to see the man. Was the best thing that happened for days and weeks. Didn't know it at the time. And when I think about that time with him, God, oh God, I cannot stop. Beautiful, it was. Was his eyes, or something. No. It was his face. He found and filled the cracks in me, with hardly anything, only words. A man like that could have any girl he wants, and he chose me. And all the time, he showed me things I didn't know. God, something so good cannot be so wrong. And all the time, he knew what I liked before I knew. And all the time, Mum's voice was in my head. And all the time her voice was saying, this man's no good. And all the time I was saying, no, this man is beautiful.

I do not fight the feeling that night left behind. The girls at school would call it love, would do it in exchange for love. I did it, but not for love. No, not for that. For something else. To feel alive. That night, I felt alive. The old me gone and something new was in its place.

Here I am. Free to walk the world that I've been given. Men look at me from cars and I am following someone who might be him. Cross the road, past the mini golf, the rock garden bit. The man's turned down a drive, into a house, light on, telly on, plonks himself on a sofa.

Me, standing on a wall opposite his house. He'll see me from the living room. Wave my arms. Why not? Looks up, a bit surprised. Opens the door. Comes stomping over. Oh, happy me! Says, what the hell are you doing here? How did you find me? Say to him, it's your lucky day. Aren't you going to invite me in? I'm bursting for a wee. Mulls it over.

But underneath, a smile. And here I am. In his living room with smoker smells, air fresheners, photos of strangers on the wall.

Goes back to the comedy film. His laughter is the only thing that fills the room. Oh, to touch and check it's him, talk and ask him this and that, entertain him with the giddy stuff that's bubbling up. Have to look at him to make him look at me. And in the window is a reflection of a girl I hardly know, taking one of his cigarettes, and the man who reads her mind, and looks across, and flicks a light. And if I believed his eyes, I'd think he wants me here. And the doubt in me says he's thinking how to get me off his hands. Please don't say I have to go, I really want to stay.

Nods me over to the sofa, a faint smile. Takes the hair stuck to my cheek, puts it behind my ear. Says, you could do a lot more with yourself. Lifts my hair. You should make more of an effort. Feel sick to see what he sees in me. Say, have you got any music? Says, yeah, upstairs. Do you want to go upstairs? Don't know what I want. Think he's waiting for something. Think I am waiting too.

I won't sit on the bed. No, not at first. But there's nowhere else to sit. I stand up and he sits on the bed, looking all the way up to where I'm standing and all the way back down again. He doesn't talk. He and I don't use words by now. In the end, he pulls me down and I'm sitting on the bed. Nobody says anything and nobody smiles. Sad, really. Suppose it's been sad all the way through.

I must be in the wrong place. He takes my legs and swings them round the bed. I must still be in the wrong place. He pulls them further down the bed. Pulls at my legs and skirt. Pulling me about, pushing my hands away. There's anger in his hands. Says to me, no, not like that.

Don't you know anything? I want to say something, puts his hand over my mouth so I can't say. Closes his eyes. Too late, he's somewhere else. He's gone away. I wish him gone. And I'm not here. I've left the room, I'm miles away.

And when it's over, he stands up. Jeans around his feet, wiping himself clean. He has a face of sharp, sharp lines. Feel him on my body, all the way from where he is. Doesn't even see me now. Says, you're a bit of a puzzle, aren't you? How old did you say you were? Nearly sixteen, I say. Fifteen? Thought you said you were older. Then he says I have to go. Not angry. Just cold, like written words. Then he says, don't come here again. And if he looked at me right now, he'd see what's in my face and he'd be angry, and I'd be scared. But I wouldn't be as sad, at least.

Leave the room and walk away. Pretending this is something else. Pretend is all I've got. His wallet near the door. Find some notes and then I'm gone. He may have said goodbye, I don't remember now.

Orange. Orange is the colour of the notes inside my pocket. Was the colour of the light when we were driving in the car. The radio was on, we didn't have to talk. I was in the front and watched the darkness fall. Pretended we were going somewhere. It was music that was playing. I pretended I was someone else, and the man who was driving, was driving us far away.

TOM

There's a crisis in the house. It's one crisis after another. Our daughter's cut her hair, or some damned thing or other. May's not happy, but hair grows back, it's not the end of the world. There's always a crisis when you have a teenage daughter. There's always something going on, but I wouldn't have it any other way. Our daughter has the makings of a scholar.

Our daughter was born with my brown eyes. I used to say she was watching us, learning with her eyes. She was quick to spot things. I used to think she was weighing us up, deciding if it was a good thing, our life. I used to look at her and I could quite believe she knew everything already, all by herself.

I knew early on she was clever. I wished things for her that hadn't been possible for me. I'd tell her what I wished for when I held her. I think that's what fathers do; you want them to have all the things you didn't have. I learnt that when our son was born. I wanted so much for him. I didn't want him to get too comfortable in this town. I hoped for better things than that. I thought he was destined for better things, and in the end our son was not a scholar, but he got a job down south. Our daughter has the makings of a scholar, but she laughs at hard work.

I'm not so good with books, and our daughter had all these questions saved up, that came out as soon as she could talk. And all I could say was, it might be this, but it might not be; it might be something else.

My da said I was destined to see better things. He said I would become a scholar, and I believed it because he told me so. It made me sick when I ended up not being the son he thought I was. I was taken out of school early and I've worked ever since. I tried catching up with my studies later on, but I never managed to get back on track, and something's been missing ever since. I wanted to catch up but I didn't, and what I don't know grows every day. I walk past the boys I knew at school, who are men now, who have grown tall standing on top of what they know. It's the mark of a man to feel certain in the world. Ma said it set me back when we lost everything. She said I was never the same again. I think she was right and I don't want that to happen to our son and daughter.

Everything in this house is stuff we've had for years. I'd like to see something new for once. It would be like a breath of fresh air. The kettle's on. The food is cooking in the pan, and a young man and woman are talking on the television. The plates are out. The knives and forks are out but I feel free today.

You are my sunshine, my only sunshine. Our daughter's thumping about in her room. Fifteen years old, five foot seven and she won't listen to a word her old dad says. Oh, the misery! The kitchen's blazing hot with the fire on and the cooker on. The fish fingers are frying in the pan. The chips are frying and the peas are on the hob. 'I thought we'd have a change today,' May says. 'This is one of my favourite meals,' I say. 'I know it is,' she says, and smiles. I'm back to my old self again. Nothing can touch me. Our daughter comes down for her tea, wanting to go out after, and her mother says she can't go out looking like that. I want to add my bit, but they won't listen to what I have to say. They only listen to what they want to hear.

This young man and woman on TV are fashion designers, but they aren't on here to talk about clothes. They're on here to tell us something. They've been put in front of us to talk about money. We watch them walk into a restaurant and order expensive drinks. They say they're working, but it doesn't look like work to me. They say that houses are making money, pictures and chairs are making money. Even wine makes money. Everything's making money, and they know which paintings will make them money, and they make lots, and they'll keep on making more. They seem to be saying there's no limit to the amount of money they can make.

Their lives are very different to our lives here. Life looks very different for these people who like to talk for a living. They seem to be saying there's no excuse for being poor now that everything's worth money.

They walk through expensive doors and know what food and drink to order. I wonder how they know these things. They have a certain kind of confidence that comes from knowing how to stack things in their favour. How I would like our son and daughter to be able to walk into a place like that and order something good. To look at a painting, and see something more than just the trees and people. I'd like them to have that kind of confidence where you know you'll always land on your feet.

On the television, we've been left out in the street looking in at people who are making money and talking about money. They seem to think we can learn lots from them. I look at our room, and know for a fact we're not sitting on chairs that could make us money. That picture of a cottage won't fetch money, and houses round here aren't worth what people paid ten years ago. I look at our room and wonder what those two would say if they came in here. I look at our room and I'd like to see something else. The things in our house let us down. I'd like to think we had more taste than this.

I pull up the paper and think about our daughter. I don't want to put pressure on her; I feel pressure all the time, and pressure doesn't work. I've pulled up the paper and I'm thinking about the future. I want our daughter to have a future, the kind we've just seen on the television. Behind the paper, I think about patience. Patience is better than pressure. May says we don't push our daughter enough. But I say, when you push someone, they push you back. And when you push them hard, they bend, and then they break. Behind the paper, I think I should say something to our daughter, but she won't listen to me. I think it hits young people hard if things go against them. It can change their mindset if they believe they're not valued, they're not worth much. I'm behind the paper now, thinking about failure. What it feels like when things go against you, how much it sets you back.

Our daughter ate with us, then she stayed at the table and helped put the pots away. Something must be wrong. Our daughter came in the living room and now she's sitting with us watching TV. She must be up to something. She kept her promise and stayed in for once. And she stayed in the night before. It's been like this since she cut her hair. Our daughter, fifteen going on twenty-five, thinks she knows everything and we know nothing. What a terrible thing it will be if our daughter leaves school and there's nothing out there for her. It will be a terrible thing if she believes she has no future. That's when young people start getting into trouble. You see it all the time round here.

The football's on, but I'm thinking about something else. I'm trying to watch the football, but I'm thinking about the future. I want our daughter to have a purpose and a future. Those lads who play football, they have a bit of pride in themselves, they have a bit of self-belief. But when you're told there's nothing out there for you, it finishes you. When you're shown you're not wanted, you might as well be told you're finished.

I saw it happen to Da when we lost everything. It changed him as a man. It finished him, and bit by bit, we were finished too. I don't want that to happen again. I don't want that to happen to us. I watch the football and I'm feeling quite upset. The world can be a cruel place if you're on the wrong side of the tracks. And I should know because I've been there and you never quite get back. I have to get up and do something, it's making me upset. So many people aren't wanted now, and it's mainly of that woman's making. You see them on the news, filing out of yards. All those people losing their jobs, and those kinds of jobs won't come back again. It's always on the news, some place that's shutting down, and you wonder what's next for those people. When they're asked about what happened afterwards, their worlds are in pieces. You hear them being interviewed, and it's not just affected them, it's affected their families, and the area they live in too. Those areas are dying. These are ordinary people trying to get on with their lives. Just like we are. And they were doing all right until everything changed on a turn.

I go in the kitchen. At work, they've only just started and I'm feeling the pressure already. It's pressure all the time. It's pressure knowing I'm at the end of my rope. And when I wake up in the morning, I know I have to go through it all again. I wash my hands and think about money, and managing on what we've got. While I wash my hands I think about the money I don't have, what we paid out in bills, what we gave the landlord, what I took out from what we've saved up. I wash my hands and wonder how we got here.

I've tried to steer clear of trouble, and here we are, in trouble. Then I start to think about trouble.

In our hallway, I'm thinking about the day this lot got in. I won't forget that day in a hurry. What a terrible day that was. In the hallway, I'm counting up the days. I'm counting up the days I have left to work, and all the time, I'm thinking about that woman. This is her making and she's only just started, and she won't be stopped at any cost. In the hallway, I feel the pressure. I have to keep this job. And if I don't, I'll be finished, and we'll all be finished too.

I need to wash this feeling away. I'm trying not to think about that woman but I think about her all the time. I'm in the bathroom washing my face with soap and water, thinking that woman will have a hand in what happens to us. And all the time, I think that what we're dealing with here is someone who can't be dealt with. I'm trying to wash this feeling away, and I think that woman must be stopped. And I want to know something – that after everything she's done, she can still feel doubt. Because when I look at that woman's face, there's not a shred of doubt in it, and doubt is what makes us human. And the look on her face tells me she won't be stopped at any cost. She believes one hundred per cent in what she's doing. I stand in the bathroom and think, that woman won't stop until she's finished, and where will we be by then? I stand here and I feel like crying, but crying doesn't help. I dry my hands and face and think about power. That woman has a lot of power. She's more powerful than me. I look at the man in the mirror, and I don't see much power in his face. You can see power in people's eyes, and the man in the mirror has ordinary eyes. They're the eyes of a man who's done a few ordinary things, but he's no match for her. I check my hands and think about strength. I'm strong in some ways but she is stronger than me. I look in the mirror and feel like I've already lost. I'm on the ropes, and I've never begged for anything in my life, but here I am, begging her to spare me. She, who hates the very ground I walk on. And I'm pleading with her to stop before it goes too far. Before it comes to me. I'm for the chop, and I'm pleading with the woman who wields the axe, who thinks that things are solved by cutting things out and chopping things off. She has an axe in her hand, and every day she chops and cuts. And she's coming for me. And I'm not ready. I'm not prepared.

I go downstairs and pretend we're not in danger. I go downstairs and pretend there's nothing wrong. I don't want my wife and daughter worrying, I worry enough for all of us. I sit in my chair and drink my tea. I don't want May to know what I'm thinking. She wouldn't want to know what's in my head.

I sit in my chair and tell myself we'll be all right. It's meant to work. It's something you can say and it's meant to work. It's meant to make you feel better, and I don't believe a word of it. I sit in this chair and so many things are going round my head. I sit here and wonder how long I can stand this pressure. How long I can go on like this. I sit here and wonder if I can keep going. I sit here and think, what will be, will be. I feel so upset, I just want it all to stop. I sit here and think, tomorrow's another day. I just have to get through this last hour without my wife and daughter noticing, then I can go to sleep. I look at these two sitting here and they are my world. I think about them all the time. Meeting May and having a family is the one thing I'm proud to say I've done. I look at them and think, keep going. Keep going for them. And that seems to do the trick. I look at them and feel a bit happier than I have done for quite some time.

MAGGIE

Cut my hair with sewing scissors. Cut out the girl to show the woman underneath. There is anger over this and skirts, and going out, my clatter footsteps coming in at night. She's on red alert, looking into every corner of me. I am madam, I am minx. Says, don't you think about bringing a surprise home with you, 'cos you'd get yourself thrown out. Measuring me with measuring eyes. Say to her, what do you mean? Says, you know very well what I mean. If you bring a baby home, we won't be dealing with it. Say, you'd throw me out? Me and your grandchild? Says, yes, we would. You'll be on your own if you pull a stunt like that. Say, why would you do that? Says, you know full well why. I don't. Are you bothered about what the neighbours would think? Laugh in her face because the world will go on without her. But I could cry that she would leave me high and dry. There's no love in her. There's fire in my head. It's fire all the time. And the fire feels dangerous, the fire feels good.

Took two nights to pierce my ears. Pushed some earrings through. Earrings I swapped for something. Lopsided, I don't care. One day, she sees them. Says, how did you get those? You don't have money for those. Say, I did them myself. I asked you if I could have them for my birthday and you said no. Says, they look like something a man would buy you. Are you sure a man didn't buy you these, in exchange for something? I told you, Mum, I did them myself. No need for mother's, men's or money's help.

Now, I have money of my own, but not for long. Spent some on clothes. Didn't feel like stealing when my hand was in his wallet. Felt more like fighting back.

In trouble again, I have to stay in. Three days in a row,

mince and potatoes for tea. Tonight, he was talking about doctors. Said, did you know I was going to be a doctor? You wouldn't think it to look at me now, but I had it in me to do it. Then I fell behind. That's why I'm telling you this, love, because you have it in you to do anything you want. You've got your whole life ahead of you, and I want you to make a success of it. Don't be like me, your old dad. Are you listening, love? Yes, Dad. You see, I don't see anything for you here. There are no good jobs here. So doing well in your studies is your ticket out. I know you do what you can, with the extra studying you do. But I want you to stay on track. It's important, you have exams coming up, and you could be in a profession, love. Just think about it. If you studied to become a doctor, you'd never have to worry about money again. You could have everything you want. Think about it. I don't want you to end up like I did. You could have so much more. Are you listening, love? Yes, Dad. Good, because I learned the hard way, so what I'm telling you is based on my experience. I don't want you to make the same mistakes I made. Are you listening? I am, yes, I am. If you fall behind, you'll regret it later on, love, believe me. You'll wish you'd pulled out all the stops at school. You're given this chance once in life so take it with both hands and do your best, because it gets harder when you're older. It's like they say, you can't teach an old dog new tricks. Are you listening to me, love? Yes, Dad.

I know something and I cannot say. Woke up today wanting things to be different from the days that went before. Washed my hair, it smelled of flowers. Said, let this be the start of something new. Sitting at the table, smell the flowers faintly there. If I loved him, I would make him proud, and I'd never have to worry about money again.

Soon, he'll find out I'm not up to much. I'm sad for that day. Sad for him, not for me. I'm falling. Falling behind, but not quite fallen yet.

Tonight, I'm with them in the living room with all the things around us that make us feel at home. Vases on the mats, pottery figures, the picture over the gas fire. There's a box I made years ago, that's embarrassingly on show. Saved an egg box from the bin, bit of lace off a dress, shells we found on holiday. The sea was trapped inside them. Glued it all together to give to her. I loved her so much then. More than anything in the world. Where did it go?

On TV, it's football then the news. The news is his world, the world he sees. Another factory closing down. All those people thrown away. The funny way he sits and watches. Watching like he cannot stop. Any of those faces could be him. Is that the world we live in? Spat into work, spat out again? I want to ask. Don't talk to your dad. The news is on. He needs to listen. God, oh God, it's my turn soon. I don't feel ready.

All those people thrown away. It's what he's warning me about. What he's trying to tell me. And the fire in my head won't let me hear a word. Always wanting, that's me. Take the wanting part and cut it out. It does no good. I'm falling. And the place I'm falling to is dark and mad.

TOM

Life is about the small things: smiles in the street, half a day off, walking through town on this hot and sunny day. I'm window shopping on my way to work. Only looking, I'm not in a position to buy much. There are moths in my wallet after the landlord's had his whack, and our daughter's cleaned me out. Everyone wants something. Not May. She's not like that, but there aren't many like her.

I walk around town thinking how much I would like to buy something. I would like to hold something new and know it was ours. To see something different in our home. The shops are full of things you can only buy if you have a bit of money. And there are people walking about with bags of stuff, looking in the windows, waiting for something to pull them over and make them want it. There's so much wanting here. Money's everywhere, it's moving all around me. And I have to ask, how is it possible that all these people, who are ordinary folk like me, can want so much, and spend so much, when times are hard?

I give myself up to the last door, go over to the magazines, find a magazine about cars, and take it to the till. The man in front of me pays with a credit card, and suddenly, everything I've been seeing makes sense.

I was saying to May we're falling behind. I've been thinking we need to know how to use a computer. You never know, one day, I might be sitting in front of someone who could give me a job, and they might ask if I know how to use one. It's the way things are going. I was saying this to May, and she wanted to know how much they cost, so I gave her an idea. I could see what she was thinking. We were thinking the same thing, and neither of us wanted to say it. You end up saying the same thing that many times, you get fed up of saying it. What a shame, I said, but there it is.

So there it is. We can't afford one, and just like that, we've been left behind. I didn't know it when I woke up that morning, I'd be an old man who'd been left behind. But there it is.

It's very hot out here, and I'm walking towards the building where the knives are out. I walk through gate number two, across the car park, through the door, and up the stairs. One of the bosses is in the corridor but he doesn't let on. I walk in the office where the fun and games have started. I walk over to my chair, open the window, and a pile of forms is sitting on my desk. I hear Marion saying, 'I'd like to go abroad but I've never flown before. I'd be a bit scared flying on my own.'

Before I pick up a form, I say to myself, this isn't a hard job, it's not an important job, so just do your job. Tick the boxes, take the calls, join in the conversation, have your lunch, leave on time, and don't think too much. It's hot in the office and Roy's not at his desk. Fourteen people, with one off sick, are doing their best to keep their jobs and keep things pleasant. I think we're doing very well.

I answer the phone and check the forms and I'm doing well for time. I look out of the window and steal a few moments from the bosses. There's not a cloud in the sky. It's baking hot, but I tick the boxes, move on to the next form, and time's marching on, I don't know where the time's gone. It's not a hard job or an important job, and I'm tired and lost in all these forms, and falling behind. The thoughts have started. They always do. I sit in my chair, close my eyes and see those men filing out of yards. All those faces where the luck's run out. Their faces get to me. So many people aren't wanted any more, walking out of work for the last time, taking their turn in front of the television cameras. One day, it will be my turn. You mark my words.

The bosses didn't announce anything today, but they might tomorrow, and I don't feel prepared. At five o'clock, the phones stop ringing and it's time to go, and everyone says goodbye and drifts away. I stay in my chair and close my eyes. It takes all evening to catch up, then the same again tomorrow. I'm tired, and every night, I'm catching up, then it's back again tomorrow.

It's hot on the way home, and the heat's getting to me. I bet Roy felt that too, and I don't want to end up like Roy. It's bad enough knowing they've got their eyes on me, and there are no more jobs if this one goes. It's hot on the way home, but what a beautiful evening it is. I try not to think about work because I think about things too much. What I do, doesn't look like much, but believe me, I'm doing my best. I'm trying to be a good father and a good husband, keep a roof over our heads, pay the bills, and it might not look like much, but believe me, it's the best I can do. All the way home, I try not to think. It doesn't look like much, but it's hard living like this. And believe me, it's taking everything I've got.

May's home, and the back door's open to let some air in. She's watering the plants. They've wilted in the heat and I know how they feel. I wash my hands and ask May if she's had a good day. She says everyone was complaining about the heat. They were all too hot to work. May says they're always complaining about something. She talks about this and that, and I put the television on. We're having salad for tea. Salad and sliced bread and a tin of fish. It's quite a nice meal, but not one of my favourites.

The main news is on, and thousands of men have gathered at a coking plant, and thousands of police have been brought in at great expense. The police look very pleased with themselves, and they will do on all that overtime pay. Some of them wear armour. Some are carrying shields, and that gets you thinking. And if that wasn't enough, some are on horseback, and some have attack dogs. And if that doesn't appal people, we must be lacking something as a society. It's a hot and sunny day and the men are in T-shirts, drinking cans in the sun. And you hope and pray it stays like that. Then the lorries hurtle through. The lorries hurtle through, moving coal in and coke out to keep the plant running through the strike. The sight of the lorries registers in their faces, registers in the noise. The lorries hurtling through propel the men forward, calling them to act, calling them to make a stand. And the police on horseback are propelled forward, charging into them, chasing and beating them. Men are falling to the ground, covering their heads to protect themselves from police on horseback who are beating them with batons. There is something so wrong when men use horses to charge at other men. And there is something sickening about men who have fallen to the ground being beaten with batons by men on horseback. There is something detestable about such unequal power. Things are out of control now the trucks are hurtling through. It's man against man now the trucks are hurtling through.

The reporter asks the police superintendent to tell us what we've seen. The superintendent says the men were bent on causing trouble and had to be stopped. He says appropriate force was used on these hooligans and thugs. The reporter tells us the police did what they needed to do, and no more than that. The reporter says that what the police were dealing with were hooligans and thugs. The reporter says a mob was out to cause trouble on a sunny afternoon. I can't believe what I've just heard, and I can't believe what I've just seen. He must vote for this shower. I think he must have been somewhere else. But it gets you thinking. We see one thing and the reporter says it's something else. And if that doesn't appal people, they need their heads examining.

I saw something different in our living room. Men being chased and beaten down, in our living room. Herded like animals, in our living room. We see one thing and the reporter says it's something else. And that isn't right, and it isn't just, and it wasn't what we saw. Faced with such unequal power, what choices did they have? Some of those men won't find work again, when those jobs have gone. They'll earn a third of what they used to make, when those jobs have gone. Those men reluctantly took action, they reluctantly made a stand. And when you're faced with going under, and when you're faced with unequal power, what choices do you have? I sit on the couch and my heart is breaking. There's nothing right and nothing just, in our living room.

Thousands of people have watched this and won't believe their eyes. Thousands will have watched this and won't believe what they've just heard. Thousands of people will say things have gone too far. Thousands of people will tell each other they have seen enough. Thousands of people who used to agree, won't agree with this.

I sit on the couch feeling something I haven't felt for a long time. I go upstairs and splash water on my face. I look at the man in the mirror, drying his face with a towel. What would you give for this man in the mirror? A six? Or a seven out of ten? He's still got something. He still has a spring in his step. I go downstairs, feeling as light as a feather, because I know that woman will have to go. There is nothing more ugly than reckless power. Thousands of people who used to agree, won't agree with this.

The questions will start tomorrow. The Home Secretary will have to go, and the woman will hang on, wriggling on a hook. We'll watch her roast under questions she's managed to avoid. There'll be days of pressure, days of questions, as she wriggles on the hook. And her power will seep away under the heat of the cameras as she roasts under questions she's managed to avoid. I can see it. I can see it!

I close my eyes and I can see the woman make an announcement to the cameras, in her business suit and pearls. Doubt creeping into her face, trying to keep a steady voice, in her business suit and pearls. She's reduced, like I have been reduced. And I can see it. I can see it now! And it's as believable and real as if it was on television, and I don't want it to stop. I want to hear her say she's finished. I want to hear what she has to say, and I can't seem to pick out the words. It's all I want to hear, and I can't quite make it happen. The woman is clinging to her job, just like I cling to mine. She's not above me now. We're even-stevens now. I have no fear tonight.

Tonight, the woman will be working in her office, poring over papers that are spread over the carpet. She'll calculate the damage, drinking a tumbler of whisky while the civil servants weigh things up. The doubts will have surfaced where there were no doubts before. The advisers will say she's gone too far, and the cronies will say this has gone too far. Her cronies will be waiting in the corridors, waiting by their phones, and all the while, she'll be wriggling on a

121

hook. They'll give her time to prepare her exit and do the right thing. And if she doesn't go, they'll force her hand.

The cronies will be talking on their phones, meeting in the corridors, working out who's for her, and who's against. The woman will call in her cronies and her yes-men, and ask for their support. And one by one, they'll stand in front of her, look her in the eye, and give her their support. And when they leave the room, they'll talk between themselves. When they've left the room, they'll let her take the heat then they'll hang her out to dry. Right now, she'll be working through the night to find a way out of this mess, and she'll find there's no way out. You mark my words, there'll be a different look on her face, if only we could see it. Doubt will cloud her face, and worry will cloud her thoughts. She'll feel what I've been feeling every day since this lot came to power. I can see it. I can see it!

The woman will be working through the night because her job is on the line. She's smaller now, she's humble now, expendable and scared. She's not above me now. We're equal now.

I stand at the curtains and watch the light flood in, and I've never felt so certain. I'm not even tired. I'm as light as a feather. I'm young again. A few more days, then we can get back to normal, back to how we used to be. A few more days and we'll have our town back, and our country back, and things will be good again.

It's morning, very early in the morning, and I can't get back to sleep. I turn towards the window. I turn towards the wall. I turn on to my back and feel as light as a feather. I stare at the plaster on the ceiling, in the quiet of the house. In this light, those rough bits of plaster look like the Plough to me.

As soon as the paper lands on the mat, I'm out of bed, with my slippers on my feet, on my way downstairs, knowing what will be in the pages, knowing everyone's had enough. I'm as light as a feather. Then I tell myself to wait. No need to rush. I've been waiting for this for a very long time. I need to make the most of it now her time has come.

I go back upstairs, have a quick wash and a shave, open the wardrobe and find one of the shirts May pressed, and take my trousers off the hanger. I'm in my underwear, wanting to look at the paper, and listen to the radio, and see what they've been doing to us since I looked last time. In my underwear, I look out of the window into the street. It's going to be hot today, like it was yesterday. In my underwear, I look at the man in the mirror, the dressing table mirror. Am I ready? Do I feel ready? Yes, I feel ready, I've been waiting a long time for this. I open the drawer and find a tie. There are ties I wear a lot, and some I'll never wear again. The paisley tie is one I won't wear again. It doesn't do me any favours, and it certainly didn't bring me any luck. In the drawer, I root about and find one of my favourites, it's one I've worn for years. It's not a bad tie to look at, it's served me well, and nothing bad has ever happened when I've worn it. I'm dressed, and ready to go downstairs to find out what this shower have been doing to us since I looked last time. I think I've seen enough to know the knives are coming out. I go downstairs and switch on the radio and open up the paper. I'm in the kitchen, looking through the paper while I'm listening to the radio, looking down every column on every page to see where they've been hiding it. I can't see what I should be seeing, and I can't hear what I should be hearing. I'm reading the same old tripe I always read, and listening to the same old tripe they always say on this radio station.

You are my sunshine, my only sunshine. I hum a little tune that helps me keep control. In the car, it gets no better. In the car, it's just the same. But I know these things take time. It takes time to build momentum and I'm a patient man. I'm someone who sees things through to the bitter end, and I can see this might take time. I drive through the gates, park in the car park, grateful to have this job. I walk up the stairs, feeling as light as a feather, being careful not to slip. I don't want any mishaps or accidents. I don't want to fall and have to take time off, and give them the excuse they need to get rid of me. I walk down the corridor and my boss walks past. He says hello, but doesn't stop to chat. He used to stop and talk. We used to get on quite well before the knives were out. You are my sunshine, my only sunshine. Tells me all I need to know. The way they never smile or chat tells me all I need to know. You are my sunshine, my only sunshine.

I walk in the office and there are fourteen happy campers sitting at their desks, with one off sick. I walk in the office with a smile, and wait for them to talk about the news. I walk in the office with a smile, hoping I'll hear them say they've seen enough. The way it looks to me, I can see this is going to take some time. This is only the beginning, I see that now. Last night, I was too impatient, and much too hopeful. I got too excited. I can see it's just the beginning. But I can also read the signs. I walk to my desk and no one's talking about the news. Hilda looks up and says hello, and says it's far too hot to be wearing a mac. She says I look like Columbo in my mac. Just because I like to wear a light coat. You're not dressed properly without a coat. People used to say I looked like Doctor Zhivago, but Hilda looks nonplussed. People said I look like him because of my eyes and hair. I'm not even going grey. Hilda looks nonplussed. We've only just started the day, and Hilda's already pulling my leg. She likes to do that. She likes egging me on and winding me up. I open the window and sit at my desk. It's hot in here. It's hot by the window at the desk next to Hilda's, the one in front of Roy's, and Roy's still off. I open the window and see forms piled on the desk. I ask Hilda what she thought of last night's news. And Hilda didn't like what she saw. She says she's had enough of people thinking we'll bail them out for this and that. She thinks it's a huge waste of time and money having people produce something nobody wants. She said it made her angry seeing the way those thugs behaved. Rioting like that, refusing to accept the way things are. 'It was a disgrace. They're living in the past. They've taken good wages for years,' she says, 'that we all paid for. Well not any more they won't. Now we've got someone in charge who's willing to stand up to them.' Marion hears her, and Geoff hears her, and Den hears her, and they all agree. I hear her, but I'm sure people didn't used to think like this. People start believing things if they hear them often enough. It all boils down to what people think and what people believe. That's where battles are fought and won – when you change the way people think, and change what they believe. Then you can change the soul of a country. If there are winners, there have to be losers. There are those who are allowed to take everything, and leave others with nothing. I'd like to add my two penn'orth, but it looks like my chance has gone.

Battling on, points lost, chances missed, opportunities gone. Yesterday's paper on the fire, I'm lost in forms, but hanging on. An hour to go and Hilda wants some help moving the tables back. She wants the desks pushed back towards the window, and what Hilda wants, Hilda gets. We're moving desks, while the others put out drinks and paper cups and things to eat. One of our bosses comes in, and Roy comes in, and everyone says hello to Roy, and Roy looks far from well.

There's a buzz in the office while everyone drinks and chats. Our boss chats to Marion. He pours a drink for Marion. He shakes Roy's hand and pats him on the back. The boss sees me. He knows I'm here, but he doesn't come over for a chat. Tells me all I need to know. I can read the signs. I'm not as stupid as I look. Come in number three, your time's up.

Roy wants to say a few words. He wants to thank everyone in the office. He even thanks the bosses, and they pushed him to the brink. He does a good job of saying his farewells. There's a card for him, and something in a bag from everyone in the office. He wore a good suit to come here today, but he looks far from well. He keeps his voice steady, and by the time he's finished, there are tears in my eyes. He's a good man, is Roy, and a gentle man. You are my sunshine, my only sunshine.

I put on my mac and pick up my bag. 'Are you leaving so soon, Tommy? You're usually the last one here.' I shake Roy's hand. I'm sad we won't be seeing Roy in the office. That's one down, two to go. I walk down the corridor, into the stairwell. It's not about who works hard, it's more about chance and luck, and whose face fits. I walk down the stairs, being careful not to trip, careful not to ride my luck and change the odds.

There won't be much traffic on the road. I'll be home in no time to find out what they've been doing to us while I've been away. I couldn't stay any longer in the office. It didn't feel right. There isn't much to celebrate now the knives are out. It's one down, two to go, and I can read the signs. Chin up. Don't give up. That's all very well, but if it's down to luck, I've ridden my luck more than most. I've ridden my luck more than most people have, and luck is a strange thing. That padre said I was a lucky man, and when I think about it, he might have been right. I'm on my way home and I'm back in that place. I'm thinking about me and my pal, and thinking about luck. We were in a tank together that got hit. He got caught on his side, and I was only inches away from him. I went to help but there wasn't much I could do. There was liquid all over the tank floor, I slipped in it, and I looked down, and my pal's blood was all over me. It mustn't have clotted in the heat. I'd been inches away when he got hit, and only one of us got out. So I can't sit here and say I haven't had my share of luck.

I drive home, open the front door, go upstairs and wash my hands, look at my hands and check they're clean. I go downstairs and no one's in. I put on the telly and open the paper. And things are just the same. I switch on the radio and everything's the same. Back to the routine fear, and one down, two to go. On the telly, I see that woman's well prepared as usual, talking her way out of trouble. She's in the corner of our kitchen, in her business suit and pearls. She's walking over, and I've only just got in. She's in the kitchen, threatening and frightening me, as if she has every right to come and spit her fury at me. I can see her but she can't see me. I stand in front of her, and say to myself, she's only made of flesh and blood. One day, her luck will run out. You mark my words. It hasn't run out yet. I hoped it might, but I hoped for too much, too soon. But mark my words, one day, her time will be up, and her luck will run out. Mine will probably run out more quickly, but I've had my luck already. I never thought I'd make it out of that place, and I got to leave that place. I was very lucky, and it makes no sense, but there it is.

I look out of the window on to the street. There's sun on the trees and shadows on the houses. I don't look out enough and see how beautiful the world is. It's much more beautiful than I care to believe.

MAGGIE

Last night is here. Can smell it in the room. Remember falling on the bed, pulled the blanket over, stayed like that. Don't know how I got to where they woke me up before I staggered back. And am I really what they said, after all I went along with, after all I let them do? Turn over in the blanket. Every part of me feels broken, every part is hurting, and I'll be at school like this, and that's too much. Is way too much.

Any minute now, it will all begin again. I'll walk past the bus stops and the driveways. Through the gates and in the rooms that smell of feet. Another day of slag, slag, slag. They'll get up, put the kettle on and make some tea. I'll come down and smile so they can't see the mess I really am. If they knew, the questions would start, and they would shout to look at me for days and weeks. Not ready for that. Not strong enough for that.

Put my feet down from the bed. Hear them talking away, their happy kitchen sounds. In the bathroom, pour water in the sink. Bit of a wipe is all I can do. Then knickers on and bra. Lift a leg. Put it through the skirt hole. Lift the other. Bend to do the tights. The blouse she washed and ironed is hanging up. Makes me cry a bit. Dangerously close to going to her, as if she might hold me and keep me safe. Hear her goodbyes walking through the door and out to work. He left a while ago. Go downstairs, pour cornflakes in a bowl. The radio man talks away. Go on, radio, play me a song. Put something in between me and all this mess. A song comes on. A railway line, some lonely mountain man. Can see it if I look, it's like a film. The radio man, he says he's got to go but he'll be back again tomorrow. Same time, same place.

Cheerio, cheerio. A song comes on, the goodbye one, then he is gone.

Don't go. You remind me of my dad. And in my mind are Sunday afternoons when he and I played games, and everyone knew him in the street. In the corner of my mind he's always watching over me.

Upstairs, take off the skirt and tights. I can't go in today. There's money coiled in a box waiting to be spent. Clack-clack-clack. My heels down the street. I'm tired. Won't walk. A cab instead, then I can go anywhere I want. And the cab's been driving a while and the pendulum's swung back. The happy feeling's gone, the anger and the tears pour out. Hand some money to the driver who comes back with vodka and the day picks up again. Ask him to wait, he waits outside the shops. Slip lipstick, eyeliner in my pocket. Smile going past the till. Then into the arcade. Laughing and I don't know why. Because everything is funny. I'm winning now, brand new again. If only every day could be like this.

And here I am, the vodka and me, the money done, the taxi gone, in the place I used to wait for the man who might drive past. The sky's a smear. Pink leaking into blue, fading into black. This place is beautiful to me. The only calm thing on this stormy sea. God, oh God, those nights weren't much, but even now I'd have them back. Was like waiting for a birthday, waiting here. Now that time's gone. Not left with much. Just a feeling in my heart.

Daddy, things are wrong. I look for you and you aren't there. I've found a way of moving on. Not love, it's something else, it doesn't have a name. Daddy, I'm so far out to sea. Don't know what to do, or where to go. A feeling comes. Huge wave. Unexpected. I'm falling now. Falling away.

Scramble down the concrete bit. Knees cut, rocks and dirt go rubbling down. I ask this place to keep me safe. Down here, the sky runs into sea, the air is the temperature of blood. Drink some more and watch the water catch the sun and change with it. The last bit of sun falls on the water. Fire spreading underneath my skin. Look at the sky. Why? Why? Why? Why? Why does it have to be like this? The terrible truth is taking hold. Is big. Is strong. I'm full of hate towards myself. Feel the bottle in my hand, hear it smashing on the steps. Just the neck left in my hand. It says, look at you. Always wanting something and no one wants you back. You're everything they say you are. I know, I know, it must be true.

And the hate wants more. Do more. It cheers me on. Saying things to cheer me on. The neck is in my hand. It wants to be a knife. Says, you made a knife, so use the knife. Take the wanting part and cut it out. Cut it away. Laughing, goading, it's everything this moment is. I do the thing it says to do to make it go away. I do it. Again and again and again and again. Until everything goes quiet and I come back pin-sharp, blood running down my arms. The hate has gone for now, the sky's gone dark and I can breathe again. I'm breathing. Watch the anger bleeding out. A piece of bottle in my hand. Throw it against the wall. It's gone. It's gone for now. There's peace for now. Then I begin to run.

TOM

Here I am in bed staring at the ceiling, waiting for everything to begin again. I know this time of day by now, when the curtains start to let the light in. Sometimes, it takes an age to get here. Time can weigh a ton when you're waiting for it to pass. But the next hour will be gone in a flash, then everything will begin again. I don't feel ready.

Every morning, I get up, put on my dressing gown, go downstairs and pick that bloody paper up so I can see what they've been doing to us since I looked last time. I'll make some tea and read the headlines and the front page, in the silence of the house. Then I'll go through them again, because when you're tired, you tend to miss things.

I hear the letterbox go. Here we go. It's starting again. Here I am again, I don't feel ready. It would be wonderful if someone said I didn't have to go in. If someone told me it's Saturday today, not Friday. I think the same thing every day, and here I am again. It's time to start again.

In the bathroom, I brush my teeth. I'm careful with the toothpaste, I don't want to put too much on the brush. I'm careful not to waste things. I won't wear shoes in the house then the landlord won't come asking me to pay for carpets if these wear out.

My sister has a few things to say about all this. One of the things she teases me about is being careful with money. I say, teases, but she jokes about me in front of people, and that's a different thing. I hear a tone in her voice, and I know there's something a bit nasty included with her words. My sister's the youngest of us all. She might not remember what I remember, so she gets to laugh and tell people what I'm like with money. I saw things I can't forget. I remember when we had to leave the house. We didn't know it at the time, but it would sink my da, and it would sink the rest of us too.

I found the rags someone had put through our door. They'd been smeared with filthy stuff so we'd know exactly what they thought of us and they didn't have to say a word. I took them out and burned them before anyone saw. If you lost your money, it was seen in an immoral way back then. One day we walked away. There's a turn you can make on the road, and we never made that turn again. What I thought was our house, wasn't ours any more, and everything we thought was ours, wasn't ours any more. It shouldn't have come to that, but there it is.

There's a lot more I could say. Life changed, and we learned to do without. So I keep a check on myself as much as I can. I'll never forget what it was like when we lost everything, and I don't want us to go through that experience. I wash my hands and wonder how we got here. We've always been so careful. We've tried to steer clear of trouble, yet here we are, in trouble.

May's up, and I'm looking for a shirt. My suit's laid out on the bed. I go over to the dressing table, open the drawer and take out a tie, go to the mirror and put on the tie. When I'm dressed, I check my hair, trousers, jacket, shirt, tie. All present and correct. The man in the mirror, is he present and correct? Is he ready? No, he's bloody not. I go downstairs and sit in the kitchen till it's time to go. Last night, May said there would be nothing to worry about, but that's easy for her to say.

I give May a kiss when she comes downstairs. There's no sound coming from our daughter's room, but that girl can sleep till the cows come home. Nearly sixteen, and she thinks she knows better than everyone. I'm not bothered about checking the paper this morning and I haven't switched on the radio. I put out the placemats instead, the ones with the cars on, the ones we got with petrol tokens. Then I put out the knives and forks. I go to the drawer and get the spoons and put them out on the table. There'll be less work to do for tonight's meal. May says she hopes I have a good day and I hope she has a good day too.

When I met May, her family ran a shop. It closed, and they opened a chip shop, and that closed too. Her father was a councillor and ended up being important in the town. He wanted you to think he was a good man but I always thought he was a stern man, but not bad in his own way. When I met May, she was quite innocent of the world. She'd go dancing with friends her dad had chosen for her. They weren't real friends. I'd see her standing at the side all alone, and I felt for her, being on her own like that. She didn't dance with men very much. I've no idea why she danced with me. I used to think her family wouldn't like it if she was seen talking to men. They had their ways. My family thought hers were a miserable lot, but my family liked to enjoy themselves when there was money about. They liked parties and the good things in life, and thought money was for spending. When May and I became a team, she didn't like what I did with money so she took over that side of things.

I surprised everyone, getting in with May. The women I'd known before were nothing like her. I saw something different in May, and it's been very good for us, as things have turned out.

I take my coat out of the hall cupboard and put it on. I have the car keys ready in my hand. People are on their way to work, waiting for buses, driving in. I keep thinking it shouldn't have come to this, but there it is. That's the worst part about it. It's all about luck, and whose face fits. I drive through the gates, park in front of the building, see everyone going into work, walking through the doors. Some of their faces are familiar. I've worked with them, and they've moved up now. Some of them have their own offices, moved on to better things. All these people will have eaten their breakfasts, picked up their keys, put on their coats, so they can walk through these gates, through the doors, up the staircase, and begin again. Just like they did yesterday. Here we are again today.

I walk up the stairs at the same time as I did yesterday and pass the same people on my way to the office. Here we are again. Through the door. Bag down, coat off. Sitting at my desk. Am I ready?

Den comes over. Den wants a quiet word. Dennis Burns, whose face looks as serious as blackmail. Den takes me off to one side, and tells me he's seen our daughter hanging around the traffic lights. He says our daughter waves at men in cars. He saw our daughter get in a car and drive away. A man was driving. There's a look in Den's eye that I don't like. He says some girls grow up too quickly; they act much older than they are. That's what Dennis says. He wanted to tell me because once a girl gets a reputation, it's hard to shake. That's the way Dennis sees the world. And there's that look in his eye that I don't like. A look that judges my daughter, and judges me. What a day this is turning out to be. I tell Dennis to keep his nose out of my business, and keep his eye on his own brood. Then he goes back to his desk, and I go back to mine.

At my desk, I think about our daughter and I feel quite upset. I'd protect her from everything if I could, but she won't take that from me. I have to let her grow up, and that's not an easy thing to do. At my desk, I try and put what Dennis Burns said to the back of my mind. Sitting at my desk, I look out of the window and watch someone walk across the car park. I wonder where they're going at this time of day. At my desk, I think about the hopes and dreams I have for our daughter. You try to be a good father, and you only want what's best for them, then you have to accept them as they are, and that they're going to go their own way. And that's a hard thing to learn. And it's a hard thing to accept, but you can't live someone's life for them. They don't understand the lessons you're trying to pass on. They won't see the world that you see. I sit at the desk and fear creeps in, and so do the doubts. Fear creeps up on me all the time. It becomes a habit that can sink you. And when you're sinking, those who rely on you are sinking too. I sit at the window and wonder how things will pan out.

I sit at this desk thinking about what I'm going to say. There are things I want to say, and things I would say if I was a braver man. I sit here, writing things down that might be useful, writing things down then changing my mind. I sit here and look out of the window. I didn't think it would be like this. It shouldn't have come to this, but there it is. I go to the toilets and look in the mirror, and try to look calm. You are my sunshine, my only sunshine. I have to look calm because it's my turn now.

At quarter past five, the door to the office closes, banging and echoing. I walk down the stairs and my eyes are filling up. I can't see properly, so better be careful. Don't want to trip and fall. 'What are you going to do with yourself now, Tommy?' The wheels go round and round. 'I'm sad to see you go.' 'This place won't be the same without you.' Round and round they go, the wheels. 'Tommy, what are we going to do when we need one of your opinions?' Round and round go the thoughts. 'We'll miss you and the way your mind works.' Tonight, I got out early and left a pile of forms on the desk.

One foot goes in front of the other, my eyes are on the ground. I'm out of the door, stepping out of these shoes. It's my turn now, and it's just me, there aren't hundreds walking out with me. There are no television cameras filming me. I haven't made the news. One foot goes in front of the other, and my eyes are filling up. I'm breathing in and breathing out, my eyes are burning. Pull my shoulders back, keep my chin up, but I'm a hundred feet down, where no one can find me. There are too many thoughts pulling me in different directions. So many things I haven't worked out yet. There's a card in my pocket, organised by Hilda. It's something to look at when I get home. It's nice to have something to remember them by when I get home. All their hands were held out. I was very touched. It was hard shaking all those hands. The boss held out his hand and I felt my eyes burning. I tried to keep my voice steady. I said what I could. I tried to look calm. I remembered to smile. This will be something I will always remember. The day they took the pressure off. Now, I'm going home, and back to May. Chin up. Chin up.

I can watch television and sleep well tonight. I can watch all the things I want to watch. I don't have to read the paper or watch the news, and things will go back to the way they were, before the knives were out. Tonight, I'll sleep soundly in our bed. I won't be sitting up in the kitchen, worrying and working, preparing for tomorrow. It shouldn't have come to this, but there it is.

I drive home, get out of the car, open the door, and May wants to know how it went. Tea comes and goes. I don't know what we ate, and I don't know what we said, and I can't remember what was on the news. Our daughter went out and I didn't say a word. The television's on, the card is up on the mantelpiece. May must have said she was going to bed, and I'm still here, deep underground where nothing can touch me. It's dark down here, I'm a long way down, and I can't pull myself out. I can't do that yet.

I'm right at the bottom and I don't feel a thing. Everyone else is miles away. Nothing can happen to me while I'm a hundred feet down, and that's how I want it to stay. I go to the window and look out at the street. Our daughter's not home but I don't feel a thing. I'm miles away, where nothing can touch me. It's getting light, and our daughter's not home, and I can't get up off the chair. I'm stuck here, where no one can touch me.

It's light now. I'm standing at the window, thinking about my brother. Was there something I could have done to save us? Would he be standing here now if I had? I can see Bill in the back yard, Da standing over him with a belt in his hand. I can hear the belt being used on Bill. And Bill being made to stay outside in the box Da built, because Da was teaching him the value of hard work.

I look out of the window and Bill is on my mind. They never told me when he died. I went out looking for him every day.

When they said they were teaching Bill a lesson, I believed them. When they said Bill wasn't ill, I believed that too. I believed it because Ma said it. I believed a mother would always protect her child. After all, Ma saw what was happening and she never said a word.

And it might have crossed my mind that Ma never said a word against Da, even when Da was wrong. And I wonder if Ma hated herself because she never did a thing to stop it. And I wonder if she hated Da because she had to get behind him, even when he was wrong.

And I think Da must have hated Bill, just for being born. And I think he must have hated me for being half the fella Bill was. I think I knew that, in the way that children know these things. And this might have been the time I found out that Bill was half my brother. And this might have been the time I found out that they could keep things from us, things like love. I say the word love, but I might mean something else. Something else got mixed in.

No one said a word about what was going on, and the truth was there in front of us, we decided not to see it. The truth was too terrible to see. I couldn't have faced it then.

And it was probably around this time I learned that mothers and fathers can be selfish, cruel, and they'll do things that have nothing to do with loving their children, and nothing to do with being kind. I tried not to be like that when it was my turn. I've tried not to get that bit wrong.

I stand at the window wondering what I'm going to do now, and I can't think of anything yet.

PART THREE

1931

PART THREE

TOM

Ma asks me to fetch the apples. I'll have to get them from the ledge near the box. The box that Da built in the yard. I don't like going near the box. The apples were wrapped in newspaper and left on the ledge to go rotten. Bill and I picked the apples off the tree when they tasted of gold, where the sun had baked in. We sat under the window where no one could see, eating what was left of summer. The rest were picked so the birds wouldn't peck at them and saved for winter. Ma must have been counting them if she knew when they went missing from the ledge. I take the last three, gone soft inside the paper, and bring them in. Something's going on if we're having apples, but I don't know what it is yet.

Ma takes something from the cupboard. There was nothing in the cupboard before. She takes out flour and she takes out butter. Da is talking about good times. He sits with the newspaper resting over his heart, saying our luck is changing and the good times are coming back. He was in town today. He brought a newspaper back with him. There's a pair of boots by the door, and they weren't there before. The boots, the butter, and the flour, all came in the house today. Ma chops the apples, and mixes the flour with the butter, and flattens it out on the table. I know what she's making now, and something must have happened, but I don't know what that is yet.

The boots could only fit Da, but he wears shoes. He went into town today wearing his good trousers and shoes, and of all the people he should meet, it was the foreman from the last site, the site that sank the ship. Da never liked the man, and he wasn't going to go to him cap in hand, but money's money, and Da has family, and a family comes with responsibilities. The foreman wouldn't give him much. It was an insult after everything that happened. Damn those houses, and damn that site, and the bad luck that came and found him. They were fine houses too, all built straight and set down a straight road. Da does not look up from the paper while he talks, just like he used to when he told Bill what he wanted Bill to do. He says men like the foreman set themselves against men like Da. They go all out to wreck a man's hard work. That's what Da says. Bill said something different and both can't be right. But the worry's left the house tonight and our luck has finally changed. And things will go back to the way they were when Bill was with us. Bill's not with us now.

Ma pricks the pie then it's ready to be baked. She'll go and find some space in an oven down the street. There's no oven here. June will get to go with her and I will stay behind and keep out of Da's way. She watches Da while she wraps the pie to take it out, trying to see what his head is thinking, where it might be going. Da says no one's luck runs bad for ever and this house might be lucky yet. I hope he's right. I'm frightened of Da.

A sweet apple smell comes in on the air. I didn't know I was hungry until I smelt the pie. They stand on the step, Ma and June, June talking away in her little voice, running in, her arms around Da. Ma lights the lamp and the window goes dark. For a moment, I can see my brother's face, coming and going outside the window, helping Da, with the sky going dusk-dark. It took months for Bill to get ill, and a day for him to disappear, and people don't just disappear. 'Pass the plates,' Ma says. My nose, pressed to the table, pressed to the smell. The pie goes around the four of us, and it must be a special day because we eat until it's gone, even though there'll be nothing for tomorrow. Ma looks happy and Da smiles, leaning back in his chair. He asks me to get his pipe and tobacco. He got a loan of money today so he can have something to smoke. He takes out a library book. It has pictures of every dog there is. He lights the pipe, and we look at it together and talk about what kind of dog we'll have. Da built the box so he could have a dog, but a dog has never lived in there. I think a dog will come and live here now, and my heart is open for the first time in months. A thread holds us all tonight.

I went to bed thinking we were happy and our luck had finally changed, and we could be a family again, and I wouldn't have those thoughts again. It's light again, and I lie in bed with my face in Bill's sweater listening to the noises coming in from the street, and the cooking smells, the stink of fat, and I'm hungry all over again. I did so well keeping the thoughts in, and in, and in. Then I woke up and looked for him and it was true all over again. And the thoughts are back like a storm. Always the same, always about Bill, always Bill, and Bill's not here. They said Bill was tired. That's what they said. But I think Bill was ill. That's what I think now. If Bill was tired, we would have shared the bed, and I wasn't allowed in the room. I went in the room and Bill was lying there like a ghost, coughing and sweating, asking for nothing, and wanting nothing. In the end, he said he'd be all right if he could get some sleep, but he'd been asleep for days. 'I'll get a cloth for your head,' I said. 'Just let me rest,' he said, 'I'll be up again tomorrow.' But he didn't get up. He went away and didn't come back.

And there's something else. They were talking behind the door. Da said he didn't want people coming in the house, especially not doctors that cost money and brought bad luck with them. Then I think Ma said, 'He's more like his old self today. By the time a doctor comes, he'll be sitting up again.' I'm trying to set things straight. Bill holds the largest part of me. Now, we must not say his name. We don't talk about him, and we can't think about him, and I think about him all the time. They say I think about things too much. But things don't fit as they've been told to me.

Ma calls me from the other room but I make no move. They're chatting in the street, a joke going from door to door, the word they like to say about us, who we are and why we're here. Ma calls again. Sometimes, I wish things were like they used to be, when we were back in the old house, and we weren't here, and it was just Ma and me, before June came along and needed all Ma's love. Bill was the oldest and he got Ma's love first. Then I came along, and it was me and her, me sitting on her knee, and I was with her all the time. June came along and changed all that, but I was with Bill by then. And Da would take me out in the car and show me the houses he was building, all straight and new, and I was his boy, and I loved all that, and I loved being in the car. The car's gone now, and so has everything else we thought we had.

I go to Ma. She sits with June, teaching her how to count now she's old enough to know, but June won't be shown, she just wants to be held. Ma wants to know if there's wood for the fire. I go to the back and see no wood there. 'Will you go for some? We need a fire later, and a rabbit too.' I've not done a rabbit yet. Bill did the rabbits because he was older, and always ahead of me. Da wanted meat, and Ma would fret that meat cost too much so Bill brought a rabbit home and we had meat again. Ma says it's my job now, and when

Da sees I've done my jobs, he'll know I'm grateful for all the hard work he does. But Bill did those jobs when Da did no work and there was nothing we had to thank him for.

I go outside, and I say to the thing that might be God, if I do the jobs, will you bring him home to me? Even just to see him would be good, for he is such a large part of me, and I am part of him. I say hello to the mothers from the street, the ones who speak, who took Bill in when he was made to sleep outside. He ate in their houses too when there was no food for him here, whereas I dared not. I run down the main street and look for him in all the doorways and the faces in the street. Where are you, Bill? I run until I'm out of breath then I stop and spit on the ground. There's wood in the park where a tree fell, and that's the other end of town. I run again and stop at the gates, and the trees lean in around me, and I walk down the row to where the water is, with the trees all murmuring in the wind, saying things I don't understand. Their leaves are falling everywhere, falling yellow and orange. They fall in the water, sinking under the surface until they look like fish. They sink further down then they're gone. I can see where the tree fell. If I carry a log all the way back, will you bring him back to me? The wind blows on me, and I wish it would blow me back to before this started, when I still believed in what Ma and Da said, and I still believed in them.

The day he went away, I watched him through the window, lying in the bed. A man walked past and I'd never seen that man before. That was the first thing I saw. He stopped at our house and went in, and I stopped watching then because there was nothing else to see. Then more men came, wearing proper coats and hats. That was the next thing I saw. They came out carrying something that looked like a log, but there were no logs in the house. I wanted to go in but I knew there would be trouble if I went in, so I walked about till it went dusk-dark.

I came back past the window and light was swaying in the room. I followed where the light was going and it swayed on to the bed, and the bed was empty. That was the first time I knew. I thought they'd tell me where he'd gone, but nothing was said. The next day was just like any other day except Bill wasn't there. His clothes were in the room so I knew he would be back. It was like that for a few days and I waited for them to say something, but no one said a word. In the end, I asked them where he was. Ma took me to one side and said Bill was in a better place. I said the words up and down, and they didn't mean a thing, and I knew I couldn't ask. I know he'll come and see us when he can. He'll take me to that place one day because we are brothers, and he is such a large part of me.

I carry the log back and put it in the hearth for when Da comes home. June's looking for mice in the holes in the walls. We call this place home, but it's not our home, it's their home. Ma says they're dirty things that spread disease. Da says a dog would get rid of them. June holds one in her hand. It's pink and still and its eyes are behind skin. I take it off her and throw it outside, and Ma sits and stares at the wall, saying nothing and seeing nothing. I show Ma the log in the fireplace, all ready to burn. She'll see, just from looking, it was hard to carry back. But the log is not important now. The rabbit's the most important thing.

'You must go now if you're going to catch a rabbit,' she says, suddenly awake to the time Da will come home. I go out and make the turn along the road that runs down to the sea. There are rabbits in the dunes. Bill and I brought the rabbit home while he was still warm. He lay in the sink waiting to be cooked. He looked like a rabbit still. Someone had to put the knife in him, and that was Bill, and the eye in him stared at us, his blood running into the sink. Then Bill went to find potatoes that had fallen off the barrows. He was careful no one saw and went round saying Da couldn't feed his family. Bill said there was money in the rabbit's coat if we were careful taking it off. Then the rabbit lay in pieces in the pan.

The path to the dunes is straight as a die, and the sand is soft and grey-gold. I kneel close to where the rabbits live with all the living sounds around me. I had to lie quietly when I came with Bill. Me, lying next to Bill, but Bill would be the one to do it. He said he'd know when I was ready to do my first one. It will rain before morning, maybe before that. You can smell the rain before it comes. It has its own smell. Green, like the smell of living things. The sea has a different smell, but I can smell green.

His head comes out first. I flop forward and nearly touch him but his body arches away, curving in mid-air in a swirl. I swipe my hand after him but he's gone, and I curse like Da curses, even though it was me who was too slow. I couldn't do it. I didn't want to twist his neck and take the life running in him. I'm not Bill. I'm not strong like him.

'Ma will be upset,' I said to Bill, when there were no rabbits and we'd been hours in the dunes. 'Ma's weak,' he said. 'Do you hate Ma?' I said. 'It's not Ma I hate,' he said. 'Do you hate Da?' His heart was beating in his throat. 'He's not my da,' he said.

I sit on the wall where our street meets the main street. It's a jagged sky, the sky you get before sundown when the rain is on its way. 'Please don't cry,' I said to Bill. I'd heard

149

them in the back, Da letting loose on him. He turned away. He was crying now. There were criss-crossed lines all over his back. 'I wish I was dead,' he said. 'I'll kill him, I swear I will.' 'Could you?' I said. 'I don't know,' he said. 'Yes. No. I don't know.'

Ma sits under the lamp in the room with the log in the fireplace, ready to be burnt, but it's not important now. The rabbit's the most important thing. We wait to see which side of Da comes home tonight. I don't know what Ma's head is thinking but I know there are questions that are right to ask and questions that are wrong. I know Bill is my brother but he cannot call Da father. I know we must not think about Bill and we must not say his name. I think about things too much and that will be my downfall. Some things are important and some are not. I must learn what is important and forget about the rest. That is what I'm told. And Ma will make the fire when Da comes home because he wouldn't like to think we've been here in the warm while he's been working in the cold. And he wouldn't like to think we've taken more than our fair share and he's not had the benefit. He comes in, saying he's damp in every bone from walking back in the rain. He just wants to drink hot coffee and eat his dinner. He stands in front of the fire looking at the log, and something passes over his face that says the job's well done. He says a log like that needs chopping before it'll burn. He washes his hands with his mind on something, opening the cupboard, looking at what's there. 'There were jobs that needed doing that haven't been done,' he says. 'I worked all day to give you this roof and put food on the table, and no one raised a hand to make the food or lay the fire.' He talks to Ma but he looks at me.

Da stands in the open door where it goes out to the yard.

He won't work for those who lift no hand to help. He stands in front of the box with the axe in his hand, his head slick in the rain. It was Da who built the box for a dog to live in, but a dog's never lived in there. My brother slept there when Da was teaching him the value of hard work. Then Bill got sick and went to sleep inside. That's what I think now. Then Bill went to live in a better place. He holds the largest part of me.

It's just me and Da in the yard and our shadows on the wall. He hands me the axe. I lift the axe and bring it down and it skits off the wood. 'You'll never split a log if you're frightened of the axe,' he says. I lift it higher and bring it down, but the log stays as one piece of wood. I strike again and see the trouble in Da's face. It runs all the way into me, and it's too big for me, I'm not ready for that kind of trouble yet, I'm not strong enough for it yet. Ma stands in the open door and Da is like a stranger now. I lift the axe chest-high. It slips in my hands and I miss the log, and Da takes off his belt, and I lean over, and the belt does not miss. I do not fight the belt. I wish the belt would stop, but it doesn't stop, and I can't hold the trouble in. I hurl it on the ground, see it lying on the stones. The smell of it sticks to me. I hate that smell. These are the lessons my brother had to learn, and he's not here to stand in the way and learn these lessons for me.

Da chops the wood and lights the fire. I hear the axe going in the yard, and think of him out in the rain after he's worked hard all day, whereas I've done nothing all day. I don't feel the belt at first then it starts to burn. I cough a bit. Don't cough, it'll make your back hurt. And Da will hear you. Don't let him hear you. Don't let him know you're in the room, there's trouble in his face. In bed, when the bed gets warm, my back burns fierce. If I'd done the jobs like I was supposed to, I'd be his boy. In the dark, I see Da's face. I put my hands over my eyes but his face keeps coming back. It burns where he put his anger in. I think he likes to put his anger in. I know he does. I saw Bill's back when Bill got the belt. Anger leaves those funny marks.

Under the blanket, there's no Da, no belt, no rabbit, just the darkness and the blanket smell. Do I love Da? Yes. No. I don't know. Do I hate him? No. I don't think so. Yes, I do hate him but I'd die for him to love me. I must love him then. I think it was a year ago when Ma gave me a box, the same box she'd given Bill, the one I wanted, and Bill set the pieces out, and he was careful with the way he glued it together so it stuck in all the right places. When it was dry, he drew the flags in pencil so I could paint them in. He said it didn't matter if I stayed in the lines, it would fly just as well, and we took both planes out, and fought with them in the dunes. We set them off at the very top and I wished we could fit inside and fly away. Then Da came up and asked where we got the planes, and Bill said he'd got them for us. And Da said he wouldn't have a liar in the house and hit him in the face. But Bill was only saving Ma, and Ma was doing something nice. I looked for Bill all day. He didn't come.

Da leaves for work when it's too light to be night-time, and too dark to be the morning. He wears the boots for work. That's why they came in the house. They haven't been paid for yet, and they were weeks ago. Bill's sweater on the pillow. His other clothes are where he left them as if he'll walk in through the door after doing all his jobs. Ma says, 'I gave my promised word you'd be up early, and here you are, sleeping in all day.' I listen to her voice, to see what kind of voice it is, so I know if I'm in trouble, or if the trouble's over. 'Go and put some clothes on,' she says, 'not your old clothes, you're big enough to wear your brother's now.' Something's going on, but I don't know what it is yet. She knew his clothes were on my mind. They were in her mind too.

I hear them shouting next door, their feet going from room to room. 'Ma,' I say, 'when will I go back to school?' I haven't been to school in weeks, I don't know why. 'Soon,' she says. There are other things I want to ask. Suppose I did ask. She'd be angry if I did. Would she tell me?

I sit on the wall wearing his clothes. It wasn't so long ago that Da took me in the car to check the site. He pointed to lads not much older than Bill, going up ladders with hods of bricks. 'It's a well-paid job,' he said. 'See how hard they work?' You have to be fit and strong to keep the bricks supplied. They'll shift a couple of thousand without dropping their pace. They have to, or the whole site's delayed.' They were working in the rain, the ladders bending with the weight. Then he said, 'But you won't have a job like that. Not you. You'll be a doctor. My son, a doctor.' He patted me on the head. Then he went back to the lads. 'Those lads couldn't dream of being doctors, even those who have a mind for it. But you have a chance for it, and you'd be good at it as well. You and your brother are lucky boys, not that you know it.' And he laughed and I believed him. He'd looked me straight in the eye, and his belief poured into me. Then everything changed. No more car, no house, no sites, no school, and everything we thought was ours wasn't ours any more. I don't think about luck much, but I think Da's right when he talks about money and he talks about luck. I think Da's right now.

A cart comes by and stops at the house, and Ma comes out with a bundle of clothes. The man takes it from her, gives her some money, and she counts it in her hand. My coat's in the bundle. I go over and we watch the cart go down the road and turn the corner. Ma says the boots are paid for now, and the flour and the butter, and there's some money left. She calls June and they walk down to the main street. I can hear June's voice following Ma's voice, two threads running side by side.

'Go away,' said Bill, when I wanted to come along. 'I don't want you here. I'm not a nice person today.' I put my hand on his shoulder. 'You're a good person, Bill. You're always good to me.' He shrugged and walked away. 'I'm not,' he said. 'I love you, Bill,' I said from where I was. 'Don't say that,' he said. 'But I do love you,' I said. 'I know you do,' he said.

Ma and June come back with a cake. It goes on the table and Ma wants all the chairs to go round the table. The cake has jam in the middle and sugar on the top. June sits at the table talking to a doll in her little voice. She'll have troubled Ma to buy her that doll, and she'll have troubled Ma to buy that cake, and Ma could have spent that money on something else. 'Go and wash your hands,' she says, and puts a piece of cake in front of June and a piece in front of me.

June crams the cake in her mouth and Ma smiles, half turned in the light. Its sweetness covers over everything. Where is he, I don't say. Is he coming back, I don't say. Why don't you go and look for him, he might be coming round the corner now, she doesn't say. I go over to the window and look all the way down the street, and he's not there, but it was real for a moment. Ma looks at me to see if she can see what I'm thinking. She says, 'Don't you want your cake?' And I say nothing. After a while, she takes my piece and shares it with June. Then they eat some more.

In the doorway, stumping the mud off, Da takes off the boots and says, 'If you live by the sword then you die by the sword.' He washes his hands and face, saying he's done his level best but he can't work for that man any more. Bill would laugh if he could hear Da talk. He had a version of things that was different to the one Ma and Da saw. Da says the foreman doesn't know a thing. He never knew a thing when he worked for Da, and he's no different now. He won't take another word from that man. Ma brings out the cake, the sugar, and the tea, and June climbs up on Da. He holds her in his arms and breaks off bits for her. She's his girl and gets more than her share.

'The harder the work, the less a job pays,' Da says. He says the job is wearing him out. You need the strength of a younger man to do that job, and he only does it because he has family responsibilities, and these times are twice as hard on a man with family responsibilities. Da looks in the cupboard and asks what else there is to eat. 'Do you think I can do this job on cake alone?' Ma turns to me, holding me in her eyes, and says, 'I know someone who'd be happy to give up his share for his da.' I hear Bill laughing away to himself. If he was here, he'd take his piece and stuff it in his mouth in front of Da, knowing he was right. Bill is laughing in my head. I stick my finger in the cake. Too late for sucking up. I won't do that. Da wheels up, has me by the hair. Spit on him. No, I dare not. I remember Da standing over Bill, the rest of us at the table, Bill eating our scraps from a bowl on the floor. Which Da are you? The one who took me out in the car? Or the one who made Bill cry at night when he thought we were asleep and wouldn't hear? Da must have heard Bill crying too because he sent him out to sleep inside the box. And Bill is watching now, he says something in my ear. Just the voice of him, the rest has gone to live in a better place.

Da lets go to get a better grip, and I get behind Ma. Then I'm at the door. Then I'm looking back at the house. It looks the same as it always does, and it shouldn't do with all the trouble inside. I see the woman looking at the floor, and in the middle is the little girl, then the man with the broken face. If he falls apart, who will hold us then?

I'm running down the path to the dunes, full of thoughts and voices I don't want to hear. I can be alone there, and imagine what it's like without them all. I kneel on the sand where the land runs out and becomes a sheet of steel-coloured water. The wind catches on the grass stems. They have a voice to them. They make low, singing sounds, so, even in this place, I'm surrounded by voices. I want to pour all the emptiness of the land on to the voices that have collected inside until they're so low, they are nothing at all. I can feel the thoughts and voices moving and breathing inside me, saying the same things all over again, until they'll be all I'll ever hear, taking up all the space inside. And I'll believe they are mine then, and I'll not think the secret, selfish thoughts that are mine, and mine alone.

The wind throws me a noise, and I look for it, and see a flash falling out of the sky. It becomes wings, and the wings become a bird, and the bird hangs in the sky, as if there was no wind at all. He's been stripped of all his colour, and given back the white of the sky. He breaks free with a yell and climbs higher, searching for room, until he is nothing at all, and my eyes burn from looking. The sky hides him well. He's sucking all the freedom there is. Then he swings back down to earth, and falls back into a shorebird's skin, and ceases to exist.

He is a ghost, the only one I've ever seen. He broke free of all the voices that collect inside, and climbed to the top of the sky, and that is why he is a ghost. He lives in a place I know about, but have never seen.

He is my brother. He lives in a better place.

In the middle of the room, standing in front of us, was Da. Looking at June, looking at me, then Bill, rubbing his hands, deciding it was Bill. The sheer relief that he hadn't stopped at me. I could not take the belt. I couldn't take the things Bill had to take.

Today, I heard my brother talking. I turned and he wasn't there. He said I had to run, so I ran.

We are a close family. That's what Ma says. And I believed her because she's Ma. Da said they were lessons Bill had to learn. I thought the lessons had been learned and we could be a family again. Ma saw what Da was doing and never said a word, and she is fair with everyone, so I said nothing too. We carried on as if nothing was happening, pretending we were a family who love each other.

I am the boy who cries for his brother when no one's around. I am the boy who wears his brother's clothes, and does his brother's jobs, and takes his brother's punishment now he's not here standing in the way. I did not make it stop for him; I cannot make it stop for me. I know who I am now, and who I've been for months.

I look at the sky. You hold the largest part of me. Will you come back for me? Will you? Please. Please. Please. Please. Please. Please. Please. Please. Please. Please. Please.

Acknowledgements

Thanks to Tim Shearer, Leah Leaf, Zena Barrie and Janet Penny at Confingo Publishing; to Helen Richardson and, of course, Nicholas Royle; to the Manchester Writing School, writer friends from Moniack Mhor and Manchester Metropolitan University. Special thanks to Alex and Elke.

And to my parents for giving me the benefit of their experience. I know how much you tried to leave the past behind.

www.confingopublishing.uk